TUCKED AWAY

First book of

LIVES ENTWINED IN KIND

By

MEL PARRISH

FOR MY MOM
FOR JACOB
FOR ABRAM, HENRY, AND HYRUM
THANK YOU FOR BELIEVING IN ME AND
INSPIRING ME EACH DAY

Printed in USA

CONTENTS

ONE

CHAPTER ONE

THE FISHERMAN'S BROTHER

There is a place not so far away as one would think, but as far away as one could imagine. In this place dwells a land with a shimmering sea on one edge and grand mountains on the other. Between these lies a beautiful, lush valley. Within this near paradise lives a man, a man with a horrible red scar. This scar is not visible to the naked eye but lies deep within the recesses of the poor man's heart. If one looks deep enough into his eyes, one can see the old wound struggling to heal itself.

To look upon him as a stranger one will see a man nearer to twenty than thirty with a strong frame and nice eyes. Nothing emits from his presence of a soft or gentle nature. This man has suffered and become calloused over the years, and as he could not shut the world out, he shut himself in.

The town in which he lives is called Redivivus. It sits in the valley at the foot of the large, beautiful mountains; a town small enough one on their front porch would wave to a passerby but large enough not to invite them in. Near the foot of the mountain, on the outskirts of this town, sits a massive mansion called Asulon Mansion.

So large is Asulon, it can be seen miles out of town by weary travelers coming into Redivivus, bringing a smile to their faces to know their destination is almost reached, followed by a frown thinking of the person who resides in the structure. This quickly passes as they remember how far on the outskirts of town one would have to go to reach that place and meet the misery abiding within. It was well known this misery never left Asulon, fortunately.

On a lovely day, when the sun was shining and a light breeze tickled the meadow grass, there was seen an old woman carrying a bundle in her arms. She walked along the dusty dirt road wearily, keeping her gaze on Redivivus, and especially on Asulon. She entered the town at midday as all were out and about, heading home for noonday meal.

The children gazed at her wonderingly, supposing her to be some sort of sorceress, for she wore a long black dress along with a faded black cloak. The women looked pityingly on as they saw the bundle in her arms was a sleeping babe. The men looked questioningly as to how an elderly woman could have walked so far with an infant, seemingly without any food or water. The next town over was a *mere* full-day journey!

The old woman heeded none of their stares but kept trudging along through town toward Asulon Mansion. At first, the townsfolk paid little mind to the old woman, giving her a few glances, and then carrying on with their meal.

But as she made her way further and further into town, and seemed to be more and more headed for the dreaded mansion—the townsfolk began to be stirred.

On the other side of town, the road forked. The one to the left led to the river and the one to the right led to the great mansion. All watched in anticipation to see which way this woman would take. She trudged on caring little, not noticing the buzz that was occurring around her.

As she came to the fork, she, of course, took the right and headed onward to the mansion. Well, this truly sent the town into an uproar. Children ran to the fork and gazed wide eyed at this brave witch, who, at this moment, had passed further down the road than any of them—in all their betting who-could-go-furthest days. The women clustered together conversing as to whether they should run and warn the strange woman of the disaster she was about to encounter.

The men came out of their porches holding their plates of food in hand while eating, and giving each other a, *Very strange but surely none of our affair,* look.

As for the old woman, she kept on her way, smiling a little to herself. She had, for a moment, come out of her determined trance to realize and enjoy the effect she left in her wake. This reverie led her to gaze down upon the child in her arms. She was a beautiful little pink mass, who could barely have existed in this world eight months.

She slept very soundly, and the old woman smiled again, continuing on her way to the house which loomed before her.

"Be not afraid, faint heart," she whispered, whether to herself or the child, she did not know.

Soon enough she had passed through the

looming gates that guarded the fortress. A very strange occurrence they were not locked; she wondered puzzled.

She marched bravely onto the immense wooded grounds. Uneasily, she looked from side to side as though some malicious attacker would pounce upon her at any moment. She'd heard tales of much worse occurring within these dense woods. She came into the plush green yard and felt a little more at ease but not much more. At last, she reached the front door without so much as hearing the song of a bird or the rustle of the wind in the trees.

The silence was unnatural, frightening, especially after so recently hearing the bustle of the townsfolk for noonday meal. She banged on the front door with the iron knocker with three loud thumps. These seemed to echo off the looming mountains at the back of the house and then off in the direction of the town. She pulled the child closer to her to comfort both herself and the child, who had opened one sleepy eye from the loud thumping, only to drift off again into a deeper sleep.

She waited a few short moments and then called out in a voice so loud, it didn't seem possible it would come from such a frail, wearied being, "I will meet the man who calls himself Master Abrax!"

This seemed to echo eerily off the stone walls of the great house and then the horrible silence again filled the air. She heard a crunching on the gravel pierce the stillness and turned frightened. There walked an old man hunched over from the heaviness of his years. She gazed at him and saw he was no fearsome master but humble servant. He bid her to come as he turned and started walking to the far side of the house.

She followed him at a safe distance as he led her around the house to the backyard. She saw there was a kind of glasshouse to which he was leading her. She could see the blurred figure of a man within the light-blue stained glass.

The old servant opened the heavy wood carved door for her to pass. She did so and felt a chill run up her spine as it was closed behind her without the old servant following. She wasn't sure why she felt his absence so strongly, he hadn't said one word to her. At least she was quite sure she could outrun the old duffer if worse came to worst. That option was now closed as she stood gazing upon the young man who she knew must be Master Abrax.

He was broad and tall, with a face of youth but the eyes of age. His hair was a darker brown and his sky-blue eyes held none of the serenity of their color.

"Well, what then? If I had known all you were come to do was gawk at me, I would've sent my dogs on you when you first passed the gate."

"That would have been a mistake," the old woman said gaining her voice.

"We shall see," he replied as he sprayed a strange billowing plant with a horrible apple-red liquid.

"You are a cruel man. It is well known among the entire valley," answered the woman, feeling her courage come back to her. "I have braved this journey not because I had any desire to see the face of a man who would send dogs on an old woman and a babe." At this, the man started in surprise, looking at the women for the first time. "I have come because your brother, who is a better man than you could ever wish to be. . . is *dead*." Her voice slightly cracked, losing its brevity.

The man stared at her in disbelief but regained himself quickly. She continued, "I must relate to you this entire horrible story as your brother wished me to. I only hope it will touch your iron heart."

"Alas, I am afraid you will be sorely let down," he answered dryly. "But before you begin, I must tell you I like hearing woeful tales in my library, not in my glasshouse. Here I like to hear more heroic tales of elderly women gallivanting across the valley to slay monstrous beasts with their lashing tongues."

He finished, brushing past her, flinging the heavy door open as though it were made of cloth. He repeated the action as he entered a similar door at the back entrance into his mansion. She followed him, gazing down at the little girl with a great fury and dread in her heart. She entered the immaculately decorated house and soon found herself in an impressive library, filled to the ceiling with shelves of books one could not read in a single lifetime.

"Here we are then, go ahead and begin your horror story. I'm all ears," he said plopping himself down onto a large reading chair.

The woman gazed at this man in disbelief. He acted like this was some silly wives' tale instead of the events that were his brother's life and eventual dire death, both of which she was quite sure he knew nothing about. Perhaps this was the cause behind his careless airs. She cleared her throat and began.

"I will tell you all I know concerning dear Achaz. He lived in Zacroon, where he made a life as a fisherman. He owned a small cottage beside the Sea with only one painting in it. A portrait of him and his younger brother as lads. Whenever asked about the

13

painting, a pained look would come across his face. He would only say, *Ah, that is my younger brother Ab,"* she said this pointedly and went on.

"There is also in Zacroon a family who has Mer blood in them. This family is now nearly extinguished, having now only two members left to carry it on. But there was one young woman who was a member of this family. She was absolutely lovely; the Mer in her blood was very strong. Achaz and this beautiful girl, Jacqueline, fell in love and were married. . . Oh, and *beautiful* wedding it was," she reminisced, smiling in spite of herself.

"If you are intending to irritate me to death with your exasperating pauses, I assure you," he said very apparently annoyed, "you are succeeding." She paid little heed to this disguised threat and continued.

"Each was and is well beloved in Zacroon, known for their kindness and generosity. They made a very fine couple. So, when news came they were expecting a child, there was a celebration. But as with most joy, this wonderful time did not last," her voice cracked, and it was not from her age. "A small boy had foolishly taken one of his father's small boats out to Sea and a storm arose quickly, as is usual with the Sea. Achaz spotted him and steered his vessel to save the child.

"He got the lad aboard his ship alright and then

set for shore, but the storm was raging by that time. The men were fighting for their lives. They were near the shore when the mast broke, with that foolish boy in its line of path. So Achaz ran and threw himself over the boy as the massive pole fell on his own back. Miraculously, the boy was unharmed," her eyes began to fill with tears as she went on. "His men were able to heave him out from under the crushing weight of the wood, but the damage had already been done. Achaz was barely alive when they brought him ashore."

She tried to read Master Abrax's expression, but he had become ever so still. She went on. "Poor Jacqueline was large with child and distraught at the sight of her sweet, strong husband nearly lifeless. He was brought into their cottage and all the medical treatment that could be done, was done. He was awake and coherent but each day, he weakened more and more." At this moment Master Abrax took notice of the child for the first time. She was awake now and quietly listened to the story as if she knew all about it.

"This is Achaz's child?" he asked slowly.

"Yes, this is Sancia," she answered quietly and then continued. "She was born three days after the accident. Achaz lay beside Jacqueline while she was brought into the world. She was laid upon his chest as he was unable to move his body. He and Jacqueline

15

cried tears of joy for their miracle. He named her and blessed her as she lay quietly upon his chest. And then he died, only six hours after she was born." At this, the elderly woman shook with quiet sobs and kissed the little girl in her arms. "But he made it to see you, didn't he, Sancia? He loved you so much!"

Abrax stood at this point and walked over to the window, thinking deeply of things only he would ever know. "What of his wife?" he asked with no sign of emotion in his voice.

"She was beside herself with grief. The love she and Achaz had was of a rare breed. Her only comfort was in holding and taking care of Sancia. If you look at her, you will see she has her father's thoughtful pale blue eyes."

The old woman had noticed Abrax also possessed these eyes. But they were laced with too much cynicism to match Achaz's and his child's.

She went on, "As the days went on, Jacqueline got weaker and weaker. When the doctor came, he said there had been a complication in the birth and tearing had occurred on the inside. The same as her mother had when Jacqueline was born. There was nothing he could do. She was a fighter though!" she said, raising her head proudly.

"She took care of Sancia better than any

16

mother I've ever seen. They shared such a sweet bond, and the day we buried Achaz, she held her daughter close. The entire village came out and honored their family. The boy Achaz saved, little Ferrelous, was hysterical with grief. Jacqueline took him aside and told him how brave Achaz said he was during the storm and what a great fisherman he would make someday; that his life had been spared for the great things he was going to do with it."

"So, she died," he stated more than asked.

"Yes. She died nineteen days after Achaz. But before she did, she told me a vague history of Achaz and his younger brother and his last wishes concerning him."

"So Achaz's last wishes were for you to tell me of his heroic death? That doesn't sound much like the old boy," Abrax replied, smiling in spite of himself as he rubbed his chin reminiscing. "You say he has that old portrait of us?" he asked turning to the woman.

"Yes, but in all my years of knowing him, he never told us anything about you. I remember one day, when he and Jacqueline were still courting, I asked him if his brother would come to visit for the wedding. I will never forget the look he gave me. You would have thought I had just stabbed him with a dagger. None of us ever broached the topic after that."

"Well then, how did you come to know the name of this *dagger?*"

"Jacqueline knew. He, of course, told her his past and how he came to be the man he was.

"She never revealed any of it to me but, being her grandmother, I knew the knowledge given to her had brought much pain with it. It was not hard to conclude Achaz had a deep wound which Jacqueline was determined to heal."

"How long were they married?" he asked, ignoring this soggy information.

"Four years, but they were together for nearly six. Her Father wanted them to wait until she was nineteen before they married."

"Well, you have done your duty. I now know my brother is dead. . ." Abrax replied, ready to rid himself of her. He needed to begin the process of dispersing the immense weight he felt, which began to sink his heart at the words, *your brother.* If only his heart was iron, as the old woman proclaimed, he would not feel this horrible pressure as though his heart would burst from its agony.

She cut in before he could finish dismissing her, "I have not fulfilled my duty. Not by any means. I have a letter for you which he recited to Jacqueline before he died," she said as she pulled a parchment from under her cloak.

"Well, why didn't you give that to me in the first place, woman! It would have saved me the last wasted hour of my life. You may not care much for your hours, seeing as you have lived through so many, but mine are still few and highly valued," he spat in a tantrum as he ripped the paper out of her hand.

She gazed at this man and then to the child in her arms and had to restrain herself from weeping. He turned his back on her so she could not see his expression as he read and broke the seal to open the letter.

It had been rolled like a scroll and was quite long. He gazed at the feminine handwriting. It gave him a good idea of the essence of this Jacqueline—elegant but not obnoxiously so, lovely in temperament, a hint of dainty femininity, and a large dose of peppy humor. *A perfect match for Achaz*, he mused as he began to read:

Dear Ab,

If you are reading this, then I am gone on to that place which all go but none return. As I have been laying here these long hours, I have gazed at our portrait and thought back to when we were those young faces.

Do you remember those days as clearly as I do?

19

Chasing grasshoppers in the meadow, hiding from mother when it was time for arithmetic lessons, trying to mimic father's stoic walk . . . Such days will always be remembered.

Of course, my thoughts have also turned to the times that were not so sweet. The day father was murdered before our eyes, the grief that swallowed mother into depths where we could not retrieve her, two mere lads trying to carry on as men.

We were so young then to have so much placed on us. Though it was a brutal time, I always found strength that I had you. That no matter what the world sent our way, we would come through it together.

I felt this so strongly, I was blind to the fact you were not carrying on with me, but alongside me. I thought we were an invincible team. You had no such notion. I wish I could express in words the pain caused the day you left me and mother. I couldn't believe you could be so cruel. I know you; I know your nature is not a cruel one as others now believe."

Ab clenched his jaw to force the swell in his heart back down. He read on.

As I have reflected, I realized it was not about leaving me and mother, as I selfishly thought.

It was about you trying to stay afloat in a stormy sea of sorrow. As you can imagine from hearing the events of my death, I now know well how you felt at the time.

You were so wounded, the only way you saw to go on was to close your young heart, to harden it until an outer shell encompassed it so you could barely feel. The pain you felt was too tragic. Of course, you could not do this around mother and me. So, you had to cut the bonds which held you there. It has taken me years to understand this and now more than ever, I see the why behind the action.

"Ever selfless wise Achaz—even at death's door he couldn't think of himself. In his sea of sorrow, he ran to save another not himself," Ab thought, disgusted at his own weakness. "Even after all these years of being apart he still sees straight through my defenses." The realization struck him there was now no one who knew him as anything other than what he was now. He read on.

As the years have drifted by, I have heard word of a Master Abrax, a terror, a villain, a tyrant. But to me, you are none of these. You are still the scared boy in his twelfth year who clung to me as we hid behind mother's giant rose bushes that dreadful day. You are

21

still that boy who helped me heave mother from her bed to the table for meals. You are still the boy who wept with me as we dug our father's grave. I don't blame you for leaving. I blame myself for not seeing you were drowning in your grief.

There has not been a day I have not wished I had been a better brother to you. I must tell you mother passed a year after you left. She never recovered but she did get to the point where she would walk if I led her with my arm around her.

After her death, I could not bear to be in that place which had once been such a happy home. I left everything behind except our portrait. I couldn't part with that.

Ab's brow furrowed as his brother's words echoed in his mind. He had always believed Achaz to be noble, but the belief was now gone. It was now a known fact. Knowing Achaz as Ab did, he knew these word were sincere and pure, just as the man who spoke them. His grip tightened around the letter as he continued

I have tried many times to find you, but it wasn't until recently that I found you lived in Redivivus. I hope you are happy. I have been told you are very wealthy, which doesn't surprise me.

You always were a quick wit and ever our father's son. Even at that arithmetic which we hated so much.

I know I am dying and have not long left. It is a strange thing to see your body before you and be disconnected from it. I now wish more than ever I had come to you and seen the man you have become. This letter is the best attempt I have left. Jacqueline has promised she will hand deliver it.

She is the most beautiful person I have ever known. Although I have no right to ask this of you, I ask in all humility that you will watch out for her and for our daughter, little Sancia. For you know what my sweet baby has inherited from me. Together, you are all the family I have left here.

You each are what my heart beats for, what I have lived for, and what I will always cherish above all else. I leave all I have to them, but I worry it will not be enough. Jacqueline's only family is her grandmother. Her father died at Sea a year after we were married. Her mother died soon after she was born. This concern weighs me down much more than the mast which fell on me. It is amazing how fragile mortal life is.

Please Ab, I know you have resolved that to not feel is to have an iron wall of protection from a world

23

full of pain. But I must tell you, you are wrong. Those walls only trap that pain inside yourself, to fester and spoil. Believe me, brother. Forgive me, brother.

If I could go back, I would and be a better brother to you. As I cannot, I beg you to take the last advice I will give to you. Break your walls — let them fall so your heart can beat freely.

I promise you, there is nothing more reassuring than to hear your own heart beating. I will one day see you again Ab, but I hope it will be a good many more years—for your sake and mine. I promise to meet you in an embrace, which will be more than greatly warranted.

Forever your Brother,

Achaz

Abrax remained motionless as the room seemed to swirl around him. He had not seen Achaz in ten years. Nearly half of his life had been spent without his presence, but not a day had gone by without his influence. He looked again at the letter and saw on the back there was more writing in the same feminine hand. He read:

Dear Abrax,

I do not know you and what I know of you I do not particularly adore, but I have felt a pity for you and

understand what it is to lose both your parents. My
sweet Achaz is gone, and I am so lost without him. But I
do not write you to add my grief to yours. I write because
something is not right with me, and I fear for our Sancia.

So, I must prepare for the worst because that
seems to have befallen our family. I have told my
grandmother if I die, she must take our daughter to
Redivivus to the great mansion there, where I have
been told you live. My grandmother is an angel and I
hate to ask so much of her, especially as she herself has
not much longer to live. We leave our daughter in your
care. I know Achaz would agree with me. I often feel
him watching over us.

Please love our child. If you open your heart to
none but one—let that one be her. I am sorry to have
never met you, but I feel content to call you brother. If
you are reading this, please take care of Sancia and be
kind to grandmother.

Love your unbeknownst sister,

Jacqueline

Abrax stood, feeling the loss of his brother's life,
but even more the loss of the years he could have
shared with him. Being struck by lightning could not
have affected him more than what he held in his hands.

If the old woman could have seen his face, her opinion of him would have indeed been altered. As it was, she remained perfectly silent waiting for his reaction.

Sancia began to babble, being quite unaffected by the tension in the arms that held her. This brought Abrax back from his trance. He turned quickly and looked upon this woman and more particularly *this child*.

"Give her to me," he demanded. The woman hesitated for a moment but realized this was what she had come for. She slowly pulled away as he took the child from her wearied arms. He looked down at this small being with curiosity.

This type of person was completely foreign to him. He pulled the blankets back to uncover her more, and as he did, she grabbed his finger with her small hand. Something swelled within him, something he could neither destroy nor create.

There was nothing he could do—it simply flowed through him with every heartbeat. He could hear Achaz's words echoing in his mind, *There is nothing more reassuring than to hear your own heart beating.* They were followed by Jacqueline's, *If you open your heart to none but one, let that one be her.*

CHAPTER TWO

SPUNKY OLD BIRD

Abrax looked up at this old woman and realized he didn't even know her name. Indeed, he was realizing, holding this child, there was very much he did not know. "What is your name?" he asked.

"My name is Marceline," she answered, eyeing him warily, wondering why this sudden interest in her had emerged. They sat in an awkward silence, each trying to sort out their jumbled thoughts, yet feeling a need to fill the conversation's void.

"Jacqueline wrote you have not long to live. How is this possible? You look to be *obviously* near death but certainly not at its door," he asked, noting her shrunken figure was aged mostly due to the weariness in her eyes not in her body.

"As I said before, my family is part Mer," she answered, ignoring his impertinence. "My grandfather Baldoin was the son of Audric, King of the Sea. Baldoin fell in love with my grandmother Adela, who was a Terra. He gave up his immortal life as a Mer and became a mortal to be with my grandmother. However, hints of his immortal self remained in his new blood. This allowed him to age slowly—both in appearance and health. When he died, his body did not match his age. This trait has been passed down through his posterity, so that today you see a woman before you perhaps in her early sixties, but I am in fact a great deal older than that."

"That's a rather whimsical tale, but it contains one major flaw. If your family is such an aging wonder, how is it there are only two of you left?" he asked skeptically.

"Because when Baldoin chose to become mortal, his father was furious, I believe more heartbroken, and felt betrayed. None had ever given up their immortal life in the Sea to live on land. To have any Mer leave would have been painful but to

28

have his son. . . it was unbearable," she said, shaking her head sadly. "So, he cursed him and his posterity. He told Baldoin if he left the Sea his posterity would be cursed and if they ever *sought* one ounce of the Sea's water, they would perish. This may seem silly to you but not to anyone who has Mer blood running through their veins. How can I put this. . . It would be like telling an eagle not to use its wings. It is our nature to be in the Sea, make a living by the sea. We have inherited this talent from the same being who refuses to let us use it."

"So are you saying your *whole* family has sought out this water, even though they knew it meant death? Couldn't they just have had a friend pour it on them as a pleasant surprise every now and then? Seems the long lives haven't increased intelligence. Of course, long life is often wasted on the inept," he mumbled.

"Not *all,* but most of us have fallen to the Sea and slowly erased our family out of existence," she fervently said, focusing on the matter at hand instead of his consistent flippancy. "Some show very little effects from the curse by simply inheriting more of the Terra than the Mer. You must understand us so you can better understand Sancia as she grows older. I don't know how much it will affect her, but you must know it at its worst, to be prepared just in case." She stressed how important it was for him to understand for Sancia's sake.

She went on, "The need to feel the Sea, be a part of it, beats upon us with every breath. We know it is where we belong, obviously; we also know going there would mean death. If, as you say, someone poured it on us, it would only make the desire worse, stronger. It is as though every drop makes us hungrier rather than more satisfied. As the years go on and our lives become longer and longer, we start listening to that beat a little more and more until, at last, we give in. It usually happens after everyone we love has passed on or tragedy strikes."

She further explained, "We are able to eat the fish from the Sea without it affecting us, but that is all offered to us. It has never been enough. Baldoin watched four sons and one daughter succumb to it. I watched my son row out in a little boat, with every stroke the water growing rougher and rougher until he was swallowed up in that water he so longed for." She finished quietly as the memory replayed itself in her mind.

"Well, it seems pretty foolish of you all to remain on the *edge* of your temptation. You might as well sign your own death wish," he answered, sickened at what he found to be utter weakness, if not lunacy. "Is that why you are so eager to push Sancia off on me? To go drown yourself along with all the others? Must keep the family tradition alive! The irony is impeccable."

"I don't know," she answered with incredible honesty. "Mortals are always wishing for life unending in this world. They don't understand what it is to watch all you love die, until you are surrounded by nothing but new faces. A long life has been enough for me. I want to go home. This is not our home —it is just our boarding school."

"Well, I think that is just pathetic," he answered, focusing on her first three words and ignoring the rest. "To throw away your life, especially to a. . .boorish relative!"

"Perhaps it is pathetic, but I would rather be pathetic than be *the boorish relative*," Marceline answered coolly gazing at him. "You must understand Sancia will have the same desire. Perhaps she won't have a severe case, much like her mother, who only had an episode once a month." He stared at her without saying anything. She went on, "Whether I die in the Sea or on land, I will die very soon. None in my family have lived longer than Baldoin and I am three weeks away from that age. Enough time to return home, leave this world behind me, and be with my family again."

"Why not take Sancia with you? It seems you are all doomed to the same end one way or another. Why not finish it now so Audric can complete his revenge?" he said angrily as he looked from Marceline to the child.

Marceline took this as a sign of heartlessness, but she was mistaken. Abrax's utmost feelings from the moment he held this innocent child were to protect. Protect her from the world, from the people, from the animals, from anything that could harm her, so she would never feel the pain and torture he had felt so deeply in such a short amount of life. But how could he protect her from her own self? How could he protect her from what she had inherited at birth?

"Sancia has a chance to escape this fate," she said. "She has her father as well as her mother in her. They each gave her part of themselves. Achaz was not from Zacroon, not a seafarer by nature. As the others' spouses were in our family. Both Jacqueline and Achaz were wonderful strong people. They overcame what seemed impossible life obstacles."

She thought of her granddaughter and explained. "Jacqueline's father was very hard towards her. He blamed her for the death of her mother and let her know this from a tender age. That's why he named her Jacqueline, which means the supplanter," she continued, "Sancia has inherited both good and bad from her parents. She can overcome the bad by strengthening the good. Just as both her parents learned to do."

Abrax gazed upon the innocent little girl, and she in turn gazed up at him. He realized she did indeed have her father's eyes. Somehow, this comforted the turmoil in his mind.

"Well, we won't keep you from your journey," he said matter-of-factly. By this time, daylight had begun to fade. He had fresh schemes formulating in his mind since receiving all this new information.

"Yes, I should be on my way, so I can find lodging in town," she said, realizing there was a long walk ahead of her. At this, Abrax became uneasy. He knew she must have passed through town with Sancia and for her to reenter town without her . . . Well, that could lead to snooping or worse. Not to mention Jacqueline's dying request about her *angel* grandmother. He saw he had no other choice. He must choose between the lesser of the two evils, grudgingly.

"You will stay here for tonight and be gone before the sunrise."

She started in a state of surprise. Consideration

was the last thing she had expected from this infamous Master Abrax. He walked over and pulled a crimson rope. The old servant she'd seen before entered the room, faster and quieter than one would have thought possible for anyone—but especially *him*.

Marceline realized her former thoughts of outrunning him were very much incorrect. It just goes to show an old duffer may have once been a swift hussar, be ever wary. She couldn't help but smile, imagining this bent old man as a young, dapper soldier.

"This lady will be staying here tonight. Lead her to the Rose Room. We will dine in ten minutes," he finished this statement just as he left he room with Sancia before Marceline could utter a word. The old man stood for a moment, in shock most likely, but soon regained himself.

"Follow me," he croaked with dignity, which is only possible in the most dapperness of men.

Marceline followed behind him wondering what life this man before her had led. This distraction lasted momentarily but her mind relished it until her thoughts again turned back to Sancia. She felt the strain of the day weigh upon her as her old bones protested, begging relief.

"The Rose Room, madam," he said, holding the

door for her to pass. She looked about herself at what must be one of the most beautiful rooms ever created. There was a beautiful chandelier which was made up of intertwined vines covered with red roses. It hung above a large and magnificent bed whose headboard was made completely of yellow roses in full bloom. Some had tips of red on them. The room was full of the breath of life and the sweet scent of rose. It had a soothing effect on her, as though she could feel herself relaxing into a state of calmness.

"The Master will expect you in the Upper Dining Hall in five minutes. You will go down the hall to the stairway. I will be there to guide you in two minutes," he turned to go but hesitated as he turned back and added, "It would be wise not to be late."

He quickly closed the door behind him, leaving Marceline alone with her thoughts. She thought it very foolish of the man to leave her here when she had a *grand* two minutes to enjoy it. Really, what can one do in two minutes, especially when that one is an old, tired woman?

"I suppose the old thing doesn't know better. Probably has never had a guest to fret over," she sighed, removing her old cloak and draping it on a large red chair. She sank down into this chair;

35

gently, she rubbed her hand across its arm. The material felt to her, but she could not quite place it.

It was so soft. . . like velvet. As she looked down, she realized the chair was made of *rose petals.* How they did not rip with her weight she couldn't fathom. She had heard many times of the wealth of Master Abrax and realized the tales she thought enormously exaggerated were definitely underrated.

Realizing her two minutes were up, she heaved her body from the chair and set out to find the loyal servant at the stairs as foretold.

"Good, you are three seconds early," he chirped happily, as if she were a long-awaited lover. "This way, if you please."

Marceline couldn't help but like this old boy. She wondered how such a sweet little thing could bear to work for such a brute master. She shook her head, as images of the frail little man cringing while Master Abrax bellowed developed in her mind. She gazed around her at the luxury most people have never imagined, or even dreamt. She had never seen anything like it before.

"All this for two men . . . one, really," she mumbled quietly.

They soon entered the Upper Dining Hall, and she gazed around in wonder. The walls were made of

36

silver which had intricate designs engraved on them. The table before her was made of mother of pearl. It was a long wide table meant to feed many. Instead, it would be feeding two. She saw her place had been set at the *opposite* end of the table.

"Won't be any small talk, I suppose," she muttered, receiving the message loud and clear, and then asked, "Is Sancia sleeping?"

She pretended not to notice his visible agitation. Her words slightly echoed off the walls, removing all doubt as to whether he could hear her. She awaited his response patiently.

"No. I put her out on the veranda when she wouldn't stop bellowing," he answered stuffing a spoonful of food in his mouth.

"You're not serious?" she asked alarmed.

He sat there chewing his food, airily staring at her, noting the sallow old cheeks obtain a reddish hue. He watched her trembling as her fury could no longer be contained in her deteriorating body. It truly radiated out of her.

"Steady, old girl. Of course, I'm not serious. I only put dogs out when they won't stop bellowing. So hold your tongue and you can remain here—in a *quiet* dinner. Otherwise . . ." he insinuated as he bit off a large piece of meat.

She could see he found himself to be very clever for his comment. This young pup didn't know who he who he was dealing with. There was only one thing to do. She placed her drink and fork on her plate, turned and left the room, walking back in the direction of the Rose Room.

"Where do you think you're going?" he shouted after her as he pushed back his chair to stand. She made no reply but kept on her resolute march.

"What do you think you are doing?" he asked, catching up to her and blocking her path and planting himself, with his arms folded for an effect of dominance, in front of her.

"I am removing unwanted company from your presence," she answered, plopping a piece of fruit in her mouth. Abrax didn't know whether to yell or laugh. He had to give it to her—she was a spunky old bird.

"Well, *I'm* the only one allowed to remove unwanted company from my presence. Jacqueline asked me to be kind to you. This I have tried to do in letting you stay here and giving you a hearty meal. I'm afraid that's all the kindness that's in me, old girl."

He grabbed her plate and strutted back to the beautiful table. Marceline looked after him and felt a surge of happiness swell within her breast. He may be a brute, but not at the root. Sancia had a chance.

CHAPTER THREE

GERGO

Marceline slowly descended the elaborate stairs after dinner. Her thoughts centered on the happenings of their meal and the knowledge she had gained. They had finished in silence, enjoying the fine food. They had also parted without a word. But the feeling felt in the parting was notably different. It was one of understanding—understanding the other much more than they had at the start.

She had discovered a chink in Abrax's adamant armor and caught a glimpse of the young man inside. The poor thing certainly had made a mess of himself, she thought, empathetically shaking her head.

Her mind turned to Achaz, and the mark left

upon her by him. And all those he came in contact with, for that matter. She wondered at how he could have affected her so much despite her knowing so little about his past. Meeting Abrax caused her to realize the tragedy behind their father's death must have been truly horrific.

Seeing how cynical and hard Abrax was enlightened her as to why Achaz was so wise and kind. Each one's reactions set them on polar opposite roads of their life's view—Achaz had moved towards gratitude, humility, and love; Abrax towards selfishness, pride, and disgust.

She realized now Abrax *had* been affected by her words and, more importantly, the letters. For him to be concerned for *Jacqueline's* last wishes. . . he must be tenfold so for Achaz's. Those few words to her before he took her plate had cleared her vision.

She recognized she'd been so focused on his fractious front; she missed his tattered heart. The details she would never know, but the mark left by them told her enough. She would leave early, long before the sun's rays peeked out from behind the Mountain tops.

Marceline entered the Rose Room and once again fell under its invigorating spell. She slipped under the covers without removing her dress—there was no need. Soon, she fell into a deep sleep. Her old, creased brow relaxed and soon enough, she entered into the space of dreams. Her breaths came long and slow.

It was at this time that the door slowly opened, seemingly by itself. Twenty or so soft blue lights entered the room. If one looked closely, they would see they were in fact not lights at all, but tiny little persons with wings—Geal. They flitted about the room, allowing their blue light to overpass each rose. As they did so, they left little droplets of light on each flower, which the flower would in turn slowly soak up to nourish its vine. This took no time as Geal are known for their speed, making them quite impossible to catch.

Soon they swirled in a circle above the slumbering Marceline.

"She surely has Mer in her," said a handsome young Geal man. If Marceline had been awake, she would have seen that, as the Geal circled her, each was clothed in a light material, much like cotton. The one who spoke had his fashioned in a tunic style.

"But her Terra has finally overcome her, the poor dear," replied a sweet young lady with long waving blue hair.

"She must be special for Master Abrax to have

42

allowed her to stay," answered the same handsome Geal, who was apparently in charge of the others. "Let's perk her up a bit."

They all nodded in agreement, smiling at one another excitedly. It had been ages since any of them lighted a Terra, who, after all, needed it most dreadfully. None of them never had done so for anyone with Mer in them. They slowly sank down and spread out, so the soft blue light covered her completely. Marceline sighed as the light softly fell upon her.

"That's right, dear one. Soak it in," said a young maiden with short curly hair. Marceline's body began to glow under the covers. Her body began to change, regressing back slowly until you could see what she looked like when she herself had been a young maiden. She was amazingly beautiful, breathtaking really.

"Just a bit more," said the young leader Geal. "Alright, that ought to do it."

They all flew up away from her, some high fiving for a job well done. Some gazed back at her, smiling as they flew toward the open door. The last of them to fly out was the handsome young leader who turned back for one last glance. Then the door softly closed behind them. Marceline was left in the dark, her soft blue glow fading out as her body returned to its aged state.

The Geal flew quickly up towards Gergo's room to report. Gergo was, of course, the old dapper servant Marceline so much liked. His room was at the far end of the house. He lived in one of the oddest rooms in the house. It had been fashioned for him and was very much to his liking. Gergo was not a Terra, as he appeared to be—he was of a much different kind. He stepped outside his room as the Geal zipped around the corner.

"Greetings, my friends," he said, smiling at the eager little faces. "What have you to report of your night's activities, Finn?" he asked the handsome leader.

"Nothing out of the usual, except in the Rose Room," Finn answered happily.

"Aww, you came across our part-Mer guest," Gergo replied.

"Yes, indeed! And such a sight I will never forget," Finn said while the other Geal chimed in, "Nor I! Indeed not! Such a beauty!"

"Am I to take it you Lighted her?" Gergo questioned.

"Yes of course!" Finn answered. "You should have seen her, Gergo. She was such a *beauty*. It's a good thing she is on her way out of this world; were she younger, I could very much have fallen in love."

44

"You forget, my young friend, I can see her as she once was," he answered chuckling. "I am very much in agreeance with you. It is a good thing I never went over to Zacroon where these part-Mers dwelled—nor any of my kind for that matter," he finished, shuttering slightly.

"Yes. Is she to stay with us long?" Finn asked eagerly.

"No, she is to leave early before sunrise."

"What a shame!" Finn said, turning to his fellow Geal, who were all in agreeance, with shouts of, "A mighty shame! What a pity! Such a beauty!"

"Don't be grieved. She is to die from this world soon. You would not want to witness that, would you?" Gergo asked knowingly.

"Not for the world!" Finn said with the others again echoing after him.

"And look, you have lighted her so her mortal body won't be in as much pain as it would've been. You have done her a great service, my friends.

"It was the least we could do," Finn said humbly, his friends answering likewise in the same humbled tone. "The very least. Any would have done likewise. Such a beauty."

"Well then, I consider this one of your finest night's work! I'm sure Master Abrax will be pleased,"

Gergo answered, happy that he had struck a chord to put their little hearts at east. "It's about time you were revitalized yourselves! Come, it's time you are off to atop the Mountain so you can be filled with the Sun's first rays to its last." He finished as he walked them back to the door where Marceline and Sancia had earlier entered the Mansion.

"Yes, we must be off," Finn answered, nodding his head to the others. "The Mountain is growing more and more dangerous. It is best for us to be back well before sunrise." This time the others did not echo their leader's words. Each was thinking about the dangers to which Finn was referring.

"Never fear, my friends," Gergo said, knowing full well what hazards those were. "Your light is far more feared by those dangers than you will ever know."

"We are off then. Tell Master Abrax we are ever thankful to him, as always," Finn said fervently this time rejoined by his companions.

"I surely will. I will see you tomorrow night. Fly swift, my friends," Gergo answered as they waved their farewell. One quickly came and gave him a peck on the cheek. It was the sweet, long-haired maiden.

"You are too kind, Eilin. Save your kisses for Finn," laughed Gergo as she winked and flitted off after the others.

He stood watching as they zoomed up along the blackened Mountain. Long after he could no longer see them, he stared. He knew well what dwelt in that massive darkness. Finn was wise to be wary. He could hear those *dangers* Finn had hinted towards, those who dwell within the great mountains, the Artur.

Why wouldn't he? He was, after all, one of them. He did not see any out and about tonight. He gazed down at his withered hands. This old crusty Terra man disguise could fool any Terra, but it would never fool an Artur.

He knew they were watching him, waiting. He wondered if any still yearned for his return. He thought of those who revolted against it. He would be left alone by them, especially here on these grounds with Master Abrax. He was always secure with Abrax. He slowly turned away from the gaping silhouette before him. He did not return to his room but treaded in a very different direction.

He entered the Rose Room as quietly as the Geal before had and the sweet scent filled his lungs. He needed no lamp for he saw very well in darkness. He stood at the side of the bed and gazed down at the old woman who did not look like an old woman to him at that moment.

She had shiny dark chestnut hair with creamy

skin. Her features were defined but not harsh. Her closed lids were edged with long dark lashes, which were hiding her beautiful emerald eyes. She had a slender willowy shape. Beauty was a great weakness in his kind. He sighed and turned to leave. He started as he saw a figure in the doorway.

It was Master Abrax. He was gazing at Gergo with one eyebrow raised.

Gergo quickly left the room and closed the door softly.

"So what was the old girl like way back when?" Abrax asked nonchalantly.

"She could be one of the most beautiful maidens, of any kind, I have ever seen," Gergo answered embarrassed at his own weakness.

"You're joking!" Abrax said aghast.

"Would you like to look at my pool?" Gergo said, turning to him humbly.

"Why not? It'll give me an idea of what Jacqueline was like and what Sancia will become," he finished as they headed off towards Gergo's quarters.

"You're not mad at me for intruding?" Gergo hesitantly asked.

"*Mad* would not be quite the word. I would say disappointed," Abrax answered.

"You know I would never hurt her. I mean, she is

an old woman now," he protested.

"And what if she wasn't an old woman?" Abrax said, stopping to face him.

"I would never do anything like that anymore," Gergo answered, gazing steadily in Abrax's eyes.

"Then why go into her room, Gergo?" Abrax asked softly.

"I just wanted to see her one more time before she was gone. She truly is beautiful. You will see," he finished as they started walking again.

"You must be wise, my friend, especially now that I am to raise Sancia," Abrax said emphatically, "You know who I will choose if forced to."

"Yes, Master. I know," he said humbly as they walked into his room.

His room did not look like a room at all, but rather like a forest. It was full of various kinds of colorful trees with a little stream which flowed through it. In the far corner was a large cave. The rock which surrounded the mouth of the cave was a glossy black. As they entered, the cave was a large and spacious area full of plush pillows and furry carpets. The walls were lined in gold and the bed was circular, made of dark blue velvet. At the center of the room was a small circular pool of clear grey water.

The two walked over to the pool, which began to

swirl as Gergo got closer and closer. The swirl began to rise higher and higher as various colors began to appear in the whirl of water. Soon they came together, and the swirling water dropped softly, leaving behind a beautiful woman who appeared to be standing on the water. It was the young Marceline, dressed in her same black dress. The dark material greatly contrasted with her creamy skin and bright eyes.

She stared at them in wonder looking from one man to the other. She then smiled and chuckled in a teasing fashion.

"*That's* the old bird?" Abrax gaped.

"It isn't that surprising. She has many shadows of her former beauty left," Gergo said matter-of-factly.

"I can't believe it," Abrax said circling the young woman. "Achaz knew what he was doing when he settled down in Zacroon." he laughed out loud incredibly pleased. "Most beautiful person he's ever known," Abrax chuckled as he thought of Achaz's words about Jacqueline. "I should say so, brother. I should say so," Gergo gazed at him very pleased that he was able to bring him some kind of happiness.

"Gergo, old boy, I now understand why you wanted one more glimpse of little Miss *Marceline,*" he said, finishing in his most saucy voice. "But," he went on seriously, "that is still no excuse. It begins to dawn on me little Sancia is going to be quite a looker and that is problematic with our current location. Wouldn't you agree?" Abrax said, turning to Gergo.

"The thought may have crossed my mind," he said. Glancing back to Marceline, he couldn't help but chuckle a bit as well. She was just so extremely beautiful. It was almost ridiculous. Becoming more serious he went on, "If Sancia is anything like her grandmother, the Artur won't rest until she is Andor's."

"Yes," Abrax mused. "That brother of yours is constantly finding ways to irritate me."

"You and I both," Gergo stated as he waved his hand towards Marceline and her figure swirled back down into the pool.

Abrax sighed, "There is only one thing to do . . . . I must add it to my many things to do."

They sat in silence. Gergo had learned long ago when he needed to know Master Abrax's plans, he would know. He watched as the mind of the young man before him circulated. Gergo was in constant awe of the brilliance of that mind. He knew Abrax had to be a great deal more than just a Terra, but Gergo had yet to discover what he was, the only close possibility was impossible.

He knew so little of Abrax's past. This

contrasted distinctly their positions as Abrax knew nearly every detail of his own past. Gergo knew there was a reason he did not yet know and, when he needed to know, he would.

"Gergo," Abrax said bringing him out of his thoughts. "It's time we call it a night."

"Yes, I'm supposing a long day lies ahead of us tomorrow?"

"Oh, Gergo," Abrax smiled. "A good many long days lie ahead of us."

With that, they parted ways and Gergo returned to his blue bed. He listened as he heard Master Abrax's steps in the direction of his own quarters. A new day would be dawning soon. What it would bring was on both men's minds.

CHAPTER FOUR

THE CURSE

Marceline felt herself come into consciousness. It was still dark outside and yet she felt extremely rested. She stretched her old bones and sighed—she hadn't felt this good in a good many years.

"This room is a miracle worker," she said to herself as she remade the beautiful bed. She walked over to remove her cloak from the rose petal chair. She sighed as she wrapped it around herself, feeling the long journey ahead of her in contrast with the soothing room around her. She felt the yearning to remain for a few moments longer but resisted, knowing a few moments soon turn into many moments. She must stay true to her plans.

She quietly left the room and walked in the darkness, keeping one hand along the wall to guide her steps. After a few turns, she came to what she knew was the back door by which she had entered the house with Sancia. She thought of her sweet precious granddaughter and a pang of sorrow hit her.

She grabbed the material near her heart as she felt the old thing crack a little more. So many goodbyes she had done in her lifetime but none like this. This time it was she who was leaving a loved one behind. It was not any easier than being left.

To see Sancia one more time, hear her sweet little babble. But no, it would be like staying a few moments more in the Rose Room—she would not be able to leave. Determinedly, she opened the door and closed it behind her. She marched out of the silent grounds, fearing nothing. Passing the gates, she looked back even though she could no longer see the mansion, which was consumed in the dark silhouette of the Mountains.

She could see in her heart Sancia safely slumbering within. Tears escaped her eyes as she blew a kiss, hoping somehow it would reach the little child through the dense woods. She prayed Sancia somehow knew she was leaving and loved her so dearly.

She continued on the road towards Redivivus, knowing she would pass through town long before anyone had risen. She felt so revived; much better than when she'd first entered this town. Her Sancia was safe —the burden of her safety lifted. This was to what she attributed her newfound resilience, which, of course, could be a part of her light limbs, but, of course, the Geal had a great deal more to do with it.

She walked the quiet streets, so different from how they were when she had first gone through them. Soon enough the town was far behind her. She was again crossing the dusty road in the midst of the lovely valley as the sunbeams broke across the dark sky, proclaiming another day had arrived.

She heard a cry break from this lovely scene. Hurriedly, she glanced around to see the source of the frightful sound. Her gaze fell upon a large woman who was running through the valley grass towards the Mountains.

She was quite tall and lean with a muscular build. She was adorned in some kind of armor, her long black plaited hair whipped in the wind behind her as she ran. She was Artur. There was no doubt in Marceline's mind. She had never before actually seen one, but she knew enough about them to see the woman for what she was.

Marceline was very thankful the fearsome woman was running in the opposite direction from her. She marveled at seeing this powerful being dart through the thick grass with amazing speed. The only thing that puzzled Marceline was what she might be running from or running to.

She heard the Artur maiden cry out again; this time it was more of a scream. It was then Marceline realized she was trying to get out of the *sunlight*. She was trying to reach any form of shade to shelter herself under.

The sunlight was somehow causing her *pain.* Marceline was baffled by this. It was well known Artur could be in sunlight just as well as anyone else. Her thoughts were interrupted by the last scream of the agonized Artur maiden.

"Curse you, Abrax! May you and Gergo die a fiery death such as this!" She was on her knees by the end.

She was a long distance from Marceline at this point but still visible and barely audible. Marceline could not quite make out what was said, but a word or two. But it was her eyes, not her ears, she was concerned about.

She gazed hard and saw the strangest sight she had ever seen. The woman was no longer a woman. Marceline blinked hard to make sure her eyes were not playing tricks on her. Where the Artur maiden should have been was a large stone the same color as her armor without the shiny polish.

Marceline did not know how long she stood gaping at the *now* stone. She shook herself out of her state of stupor. There was nothing she could do but continue on her path. She puzzled over what the meaning of this strange and dismal event could be. The recent history of the Artur was a ferocious one. They were now known for conquering and enslaving any found being weaker than them; they were the feared Mountain dwellers.

They were supposed to be immortal just as the Mer, which is what puzzled her the most. How can an immortal die, especially in such a way ever before seen? That was at least to her knowledge.

Marceline shook her head and then felt an old pang hit her. The *Sea*, it beckoned. She breathed heavily waiting for the episode to pass. All thoughts of the Artur were swept away. Her body began to tingle all over, her breathing became labored, her head pounded. She heard Abrax's words echo in her mind. *"Is that why you are so eager to push Sancia off on me? To go drown yourself along with all the others? Must keep the family tradition alive!"*

57

She would not give Audric the satisfaction of having her; he had taken everything else. He really was a *boorish relative*, she thought smiling to herself amidst her torture. She looked around, making sure she was alone. Standing tall, she wrapped her faded cloak about her.

"Zacroon," she whispered and with that, she was gone while the waving grass continued to dance in the wind, not noticing its abandonment.

She reappeared within her very own cottage. Her symptoms had lessened some. She looked around the familiar home, which was very bare. Nothing like it used to be before her journey to Redivivus.

She had given most of her things away telling the fisher folk she didn't need them anymore. There were a few things left, including what she had gotten from Jacqueline's home. The painting of Achaz and Abrax and a little shell music box into which Jacqueline sang an old Mer song long ago.

Now, each time you opened it, it sang the song back to you.

Marceline gazed at the painting, which now sat on her mantle. She gazed at the two brothers who she now knew. So very different and yet so very alike, both very handsome, she smiled to herself. She turned away, picking up the small music box. She knew she shouldn't open it. It would only make her cry, but it would be worth it, to hear Jacqueline's lovely voice again.

The tune was sweet and gentle like the rolling waves of the Sea on a calm morning. She listened to it with her eyes closed as tears spilled out. This was the song the Mer sang as Baldoin left the Sea. When it was finished, she opened her eyes with a new vigor. The song had soothed her and opened her mind up to an idea.

It wouldn't matter what happened to her after this. She walked out her front door with the music box in her hands. It was still very early, even for fishermen. She walked steadfastly towards the beach. Head held high, she walked down towards the water and felt its familiar pull on her old body. She gave no heed to the pain or labored breath. She stood a close but safe distance from the water and opened the music box. The words fell in with the beat of the waves.

My mother loved me as a child
She laughed at my whimsical ways of wild
We swam together in felicity
Together we'll be for eternity
Now I am older and wiser still

My father adores me in whim and will
We swim along the currents strong
And know our days will ever prolong

But of poor Baldoin who left the sea
To wither away like a dried up reed
Oh when he left us could he have known
His little ones would by the Sea be thrown

Audric cursed his favorite son
So all of his kin would to us come
Will he forgive him we know not
That is not our but our Terra kin's lot

Marceline stood there shaking as the pull grew wilder and wilder, but she stood firm, the effects of the Geal's lighting proving its worth.

She called out, "I, Marceline, will do what none of my kin have done before me. I speak to you, Audric, my own great grandfather. You can face me, or you can hide beneath the Sea, but you will hear me."

She held tightly to the little box in her hand like it was her anchor, holding her steady from the terrible pull within. She did not expect King Audric to appear; she simply wished to finish her life strong, leave a better example for Sancia to follow.

"You have taken so many of our lives and the lives of those we love. You do not have the right to another's life no matter its length. I have realized today being a Mer is not something to be proud of, but ashamed. I am ashamed to be the great granddaughter of a murderer. A being who preys upon those *he* deems weak. I stand today to tell you before I wither away, that *you* are the weak one!" she said as her legs gave way and she fell kneeling in the sand, trembling. "I am stronger at this moment than you will ever be," she finished as sobs racked her old broken body.

The Sea was deathly still —No rolling waves, but a perfect glass surface. Marceline did not notice. She was staring at the music box clenched in her hands.

"Arise, daughter," a strong voice softly spoke. She looked up to see a tall wet Mer man standing at the edge of the Sea with her own emerald eyes and shoulder-length blonde hair. His skin was of a different make than hers, but the color was not too far off. He had two legs and arms and wore a kind of coral robe.

Marceline looked up at him, wiping away her tears, as she stood. She took a few steps towards him in wonder. So many times, she had imagined a moment

like this. She tried to speak but found she could not—
she just stared at the man before her.

"I am King Audric," he said, looking at the
aging little lady before him. "I am your great
grandfather," he continued watching as the tremors
in her body began to ease. "I am. . . *sorry*. . . I am so
sorry," he finished as his eyes filled with salt water.

Marceline stared at him in wonder; her mind
was not capable of processing his words. She tried to
speak but found herself overcome by emotion of so
many lives lost because none had been willing to face
this fear. None had been willing to overcome it but
chose to give into it instead. This was just a man,
perhaps of a different sort than she was used to, but
still just a man. *This was what we all were afraid of,*
she thought. It was just so unbearably *sad*.

"Why?" she finally whispered. "Why!" she
aguishly demanded.

"I. . .I felt so betrayed when Baldoin left us. The
anger and hurt is what lead me to the curse. I wanted to
hurt him as he had hurt me and our family; to make him
feel the way he had made us feel. How could he treat his
family this way? I told him he and his kin would be
cursed if he left. I then thought he would come to his
senses and beg me for forgiveness. That didn't happen
and he left. I thought he didn't believe that I would truly

62

curse him, and that when he discovered I had, he would come and plead forgiveness for the curse to be removed. But he didn't. He ignored me and all his Mer family. He lived with a curse rather than speak to his own father."

He spoke trying to make her understand, "This caused more hurt and more anger. I saw the only way to bring him home to his Mer family was to take away his Terra family," he uttered, realizing with each word how much cruelty he had inflicted.

"When he died, I thought his posterity would come. Whether to scream injustice or beg for mercy, I did not care. I just wanted them to come to me. I knew with the curse in place, just as he could not, they could not forget me. But they ignored me just as he had. So, I wrote them off. I told myself they were defiling the Mer nobility. I turned away and let the curse run its course, taking as many as it could," he finished, dropping his head in shame. Admitting these thoughts out loud and to one who had felt the catastrophic effects struck his heart with the guilt he had long tried to evade.

She gazed upon him with emotions unbounded and pounding. Tears streamed down her face as she asked gently, "How could you treat *your* family this way?"

She took his hand in hers, holding the music

box in the other. At this, the Mighty Audric, King of the Seas, wept as he knelt before his great granddaughter, who had been brave enough to face her curse.

CHAPTER FIVE

THE NEW SONG

The Sea again took up its soft rolling and gently swirled around Marceline's old ankles for the first time. Audric looked up to watch this moment. A moment she had longed for, for a very long time. She breathed in deeply, trembling not from pain, but from joy. The feeling was . . . *enough*. She did not have that galling hunger for more. Contentment is harmony of the soul. For the first time in her life, her body was at *peace,* complete. The two sides of her heritage were no longer in strife, but unified.

The curse was broken at long last. She thought of little Sancia and the happiness could not be contained within her frame. She looked down at the man before her and began to chuckle softly. Audric smiled as tears continued to fall from his beautiful eyes. Her head fell backwards as she soaked up the rising sun and the cool water gently beat against her legs.

She sighed happily and looked back down at Audric. All those horrible years of torture made this moment that much the sweeter. Her gaze shifted as movement caught her eyes in the gentle water. There, coming out of the Sea, were her Mer *family*. They all smiled; some came towards her meekly, others exuberant, overcome with bliss. Soon, she was surrounded by beautiful, seemingly young faces. Each knelt as their King.

She heard gasps behind her and turned to find the fisher folk staring in awe—why, it was their very own old Marceline!

She turned back smiling at Audric and said, "Imagine all this for an old bird like me."

"Old!" said a young handsome Mer man, who had been one of the exuberant ones, "Why, you're nothing but a pup."

At this everyone chuckled, lightening the intense mood.

"You'd never know from looking at me!" Marceline laughed, comparing her wrinkled hands to the hands of her Great Grandpa Audric.

A fine round of laughter emerged as more Mer still appeared with every moment. There were so many of them! Audric arose and embraced Marceline. A great cheer filled the air from all those on land and in Sea.

Audric turned to his family and said, "I would like to introduce you all to Marceline," he looked down at her sadly, "I only wish Baldoin could see this moment."

"He can," she assured him, "and if he can't, I will soon be able to tell him and all our family about it."

Those on the shore were trying to ease in closer to hear what wonders were being told at this long overdue family reunion.

"You don't have to leave this world if you do not wish it," Audric said grasping both her hands along with the music box in his. "You can come with us and live *forever* among your *family*. Your gray hair will fade and you will return once again to your former glory."

Her Mer family cheered, encouraging her to accept. A good crowd of her Zacroon neighbors were waiting for her answer anxiously, knowing they were witnessing history. She sat there for a moment thinking of what this would be like. As she searched her heart for what the right choice was, she knew.

"We all came into this world at one point, some of us at its birth and some of us much later. We will all leave this world, some of us at its death, some of us much sooner," she turned to Audric, "There is a saying I was taught, passed down from Baldoin, that goes, *This is not our home—it is just our boarding school.*"

Audric bowed his head remembering a very long time ago when those words were first spoken from the dear heart of his wife. Emotion filled his voice as he tried to speak.

"My sweet Aimee taught that to our children a very long time ago. . . It seems over these many years I have forgotten her lesson."

Many of their songs talked of their *immortal* life here. Why even the very song Jacqueline learned which was tossed in Baldoin's face so long ago. Yet, Audric knew this world was not infinite. How easy to forget when all around you death overcomes so many but not you. . . *Pride* is a farce-faced friend.

"I long to see my family who have gone beyond this world, I long to see what real eternity looks like. These gray hairs are my glory. I have earned every one of them," Marceline said as her gaze swept over her many family members. "You have given me the greatest farewell present you could ever have given, the sight of your faces and the warmth of your love."

"We have given you nothing. It is you who have given us. . . *me,* peace," Audric said, realizing he would once again watch one of his beloved give up the Sea. His understanding was much greater this time. "We . . . .I will do anything within my power to try and make your last days here full of joy and peace."

Wet heads nodded all around in agreeance. Along with those on the shore, filled with the Zacroon Terra whose cheeks had become wetted for their neighbor.

"You must promise me to do all within your power to protect Sancia. She is the one hope for Baldoin's legacy to live on," Marceline said, squeezing his hand. "She is safe with her uncle in Redivivus."

"This I promise with all my heart, and any other family she has I will be a friend and ally. What is his name?"

Marceline hesitated with the Zacroon's ears so near. She knew it might be a bit of a *surprise* to have this particular relative.

"He goes by the name of Master Abrax," gasps came from around her.

"I have heard this name. He is a mighty force to be sure, but can he be entrusted with the *last* child of Baldoin?"

"I believed him to be trusted with the only

daughter of Jacqueline. I know he loves her as the child of her father. He has a great love for his brother."

"Achaz. . ." a lovely little Mer maiden whispered and then quickly covered her mouth. The cause of his death passed through the minds of each one present.

"Yes," Marceline said sadly.

"His was not a life I meant to take," Audric answered mournfully, seeing the pain fill her gentle eyes.

All sat in silence thinking again of how this truly was a remarkable event, and how much it had taken to bring them here together. A young Mer child with large emerald eyes ran forward and hugged Marceline's legs.

"We're sorry," she said softly, burying her little face into Marceline's skirts.

"I forgive you," Marceline replied, stroking her wet strawberry blonde hair.

"You must come see our home!" The child answered excitedly, now that all that had been taken care of, taking Marceline's hand.

"Oh, I don't think I . . . can," she stammered, looking towards Audric for affirmation.

"Of course you can," he corrected.

"But I... can't stay," she faltered.

"That doesn't mean you can't *come*. It's about time you start using more of your Mer heritage. Long life is nothing compared to what else you have within you."

The younger Mer whooped and hollered as they ran splashing back into the Sea. The little girl did not let go of Marceline's hand as she led her further out into the Sea, chatting on about her new baby fish which had got poop on her mother's new pearl broach.

"That's the trouble about babies," the little girl finished, looking up at her exasperatedly. Audric stayed close on the other side of Marceline, cherishing each expression that came across the wrinkled brow.

The Zacroon folk were running towards their boats hoping to be a part of the action as long as possible. Soon enough, Marceline was immersed to her waist; the little girl still held her hand firmly but was completely under water. She was still talking and would leap out every now and then so Marceline could hear a few words of whatever she was currently talking about.

The water felt so good against her skin, but she felt the fear seeping into her as they walked further and further out. She had never swum. Would she be able to breathe under the water as her water dwelling

71

family? Most of them were already down in the depths, out of sight. *There's only one way to find out*, she thought. Taking in a large breath of courage, she plunged into the Sea.

Audric's strong laugh filled the air as he followed her in. He came in to find her, eyes closed, holding her breath with her hand pinching her nose. The little Mer child was staring at her speechless. She was pulling her by the other hand, which was difficult because it still held the music box.

She turned to Audric with a look of, "What. . . is she *doing*?"

He laughed, which caused Marceline to open her eyes. His laugh wasn't garbled, as it should have been, it was clear just like above water.

She pulled her hand away from her mouth, but her cheeks were still puffed out. She gave him a questioning look to which he nodded encouragingly. She sipped a tiny bit, expecting her mouth to fill with water. It didn't.

She daringly breathed in; it was just like normal. She could not fathom how it was possible, but it apparently was. She looked down excitedly at her little friend who, she had discovered, was named Bibi.

Bibi gave her a look of confusion but shrugged her little shoulders and commenced to tell her about her big brother who thought he could hide her baby fish from her. He simply did not realize how smart she was.

"How is this possible?" Marceline turned to Audric in awe.

"Would you really like me to explain?" Audric asked.

Marceline thought of the short time she had left on this earth. Did she really want to spend her last hours on such details?

She answered, "No. . . No. I would like to go and see Bibi's home."

Too often her focus on such details had distracted her from the joy of experience.

Bibi twirled around and sped off shouting for Marceline to follow, which she did gladly. It was amazing how light her body was in the water. What she saw was even more amazing. Some were indeed swimming, but others merely walked like usual through the water far above the seafloor. She gazed around at the numerous colorful fish who greeted her like a pet dog would. She suddenly felt bad for the many fish she had eaten. She soothed her conscience that none of them were like this colorful bunch.

Audric soared through the water zig- zagging back and forth as he swam. Many of her Mer family came around her, telling her how good she was doing.

They suggested getting better clothing for Marceline. She just laughed and then noticed their feet were webbed and a clear kind of webbing was between their fingers.

She thought back and knew Audric and Bibi hadn't had this when they were above water. She looked down at her own hands and let out a cry. The same clear webbing was between her own fingers and her skin was now the same make as theirs. The others laughed as she showed them, as though they didn't already know. She quickly began removing her shoes and stockings, and, sure enough, her own feet were changed. They were much more flat and wide, with connected toes. No wonder her shoes pinched as she removed them.

I was wondering when you would remove those," a lovely auburn haired Mer lady said, swimming up alongside her and then began walking. "I'm Bibi's mother, my name is Veva."

"How is your new broach doing?" Marceline smiled.

"Oh *my*, she would tell you *that* story?" Veva chuckled. "I knew she wasn't ready for a baby fish yet. Her father insisted," she finished, shaking her head.

"Is that what your pets are down here? Fish?"

"Yes, often, but not always. We also have some

animals I'm sure you'll be surprised to see," Veva smiled knowingly.

"What do you mean?" Marceline inquired curiously.

Veva pointed off to the left of them, Marceline turned and her mouth fell open. There was a man riding upon a horse. Not like the horses you find on land but quite similar. It was purple and yellow, and its mane and tail were more like chords than hair. Its skin was glossy with no soft fur covering its body. Every other feature was in accordance with the land breed. It was strange but beautiful, and very fast. The Mer man galloped past them smiling triumphantly at her befuddled expression.

"What do you call those?" Marceline asked.

"Cheval," Bibi answered before her mother could, "Aren't they pretty?"

"Yes they are and very *surprising*," Marceline said smiling to Veva.

"We're getting close to our house now," Bibi chirped. "Come on!"

Marceline looked ahead to where Bibi was hurrying and saw an underwater city—*much* larger than Redivivus, let alone her little Zacroon. The houses were large and made of a kind of beautiful white smooth stone. Each was crowned with amazing roofs, some

75

adorned in waving seaweed, while others were shells of amazing colors. The uniqueness of all was overwhelming to a newcomer's senses.

But what was most impressive was the castle at the center of it all. She was amazed she hadn't noticed it a long time before. The houses all expanded out around it, with yards as distinct as their roofs, she noted.

The castle was massive and made entirely of mother of pearl, causing everything around it to shimmer. It had a large twisting emerald spiral which came out of the tallest tower. The smaller towers also had smaller twisting spirals, some made of ruby, others sapphire, a few amethyst, fewer opal, and the two smallest were yellow topaz.

"What do you think?" Audric said, having not missed a moment.

"I'm not sure my mind *is* thinking anymore," Marceline laughed, amazed at this exotic world which had been right under her nose her whole life. "It is even more beautiful than in my dreams."

"There is much more to see and many more things to discuss," he smiled, taking her by the arm.

"But first you have to see my house," Bibi said, taking her other arm.

"It's that one," she smiled proudly, pointing at a lovely one with yellow, green, and blue coral all over the roof and two tall seaweed bushes happily waving by the front door.

"It's beautiful!" Marceline said wide-eyed for added effect. Bibi was perfectly pleased with her reaction and skipped off to go and find her baby fish to show Marceline, he was even *more* impressive.

Audric led her towards the Castle as they were waved at, or called out to, or accompanied by her large family.

Inside the Castle was a great Throne Room with large twisted emerald pillars. The walls were made of gigantic pale blue shells. Audric led Marceline to the center of the room where a large emerald circle lay in its floor. A great many of the Mer had entered this hall and were standing or floating along the sides. The room was silent, and a somber mood was felt distinctly.

"It was on this spot so long ago I cursed Baldoin, and it was in this place many of you here sang a song as he bid farewell. We now have here with us Marceline, the legacy of Baldoin. She holds that song in her hands," he then turned to Marceline, "Open the box."

She slowly opened the box, not sure whether it would work or not. At this point, it would not be the strangest happenings of the day. Jacqueline's beautiful voice filled the room and pierced each heart.

My mother loved me as a child
She laughed at my whimsical ways of wild
We swam together in felicity
Together we'll be for eternity

Now I am older and wiser still
My father adores me in whim and will
We swim along the currents strong
And know our days will ever prolong

But of poor Baldoin who left the sea
To wither away like a dried up reed
Oh when he left us could he have known
His little ones would by the Sea be thrown

Audric cursed his favorite son
So all of his kin would to us come
Will he forgive him we know not
That is not our but our Terra kin's lot

As the last words finished more than many had
bowed heads, covered faces, and shame-filled hearts.
Marceline closed the shell box and was trying to control
her own emotions. Audric stared with a furrowed brow

78

at the spot on the floor where Baldoin once stood. Picturing the son he'd lost by trying to clench. Marceline saw the tears that slid down his face did not mix with the Sea until they fell from the skin.

"May I see the box?" he asked softly. Marceline was surprised but put the box slowly into his hand. He set it down on the spot at which he stared, and the little box began to shine. It was so bright; they all shielded their eyes and then the bright light subsided. The little box was no longer made of shells but was now a beautiful emerald box with intricate silver designs throughout. Audric picked it up and handed it back to Marceline gently. She noticed the heaviness of this new box.

"Open it," he said softly. Marceline obeyed and once again, Jacqueline's voice filled the room, but created a much different effect.

My mother loved me as a child
She taught me goodness so gentle and mild
We swim here together in felicity
One day we will for eternity

Now I am older and wiser still
My father guides my heart to feel
We swim along the currents strong
When this world dies we'll still prolong

79

And of Baldoin who left the Sea

His blood runs strong in his posterity

Oh when he left us could he have known

The lesson to us that would be shown

Audric forgave his precious son

So all of his kin could to us come

In love we have all been brought

Terra and Mer together wrought

Marceline closed the new box and looked around to see a room full of rolling teary eyes. She put her arm around Audric, who was very much affected. She looked down at the box thoughtfully. The pain which was the old song had been replaced by the mending of the new. This New Song marked the beginning of a new day for the noble Mer.

CHAPTER SIX

NO DISGUISE

Abrax woke later than usual and rushed to the little bassinet he'd formed out of a large basket and pillows. He gazed down at the sweet little sleeping face and bent forward to gain a closer look. Sunlight was filtering into the room through his large glass veranda doors. He saw with a fright it would soon reach Sancia. This would not do. Panic struck as he quickly, and as quietly as he could, grabbed a blanket from the foot of his bed and tried to cover the door. Finding the task impossible, he cursed the formerly loved doors.

He then decided the only other option would be moving the basket as gently as he could without stirring her. He knew this was a precarious route, but he could not stop the sun. He crouched down and eased the basket off the table where it sat, keeping his eyes glued on Sancia to see if she stirred at all. Nothing. He slowly walked over to his bed, taking an almost ridiculous amount of time. The child's little open mouth didn't even twitch. He gently rested the basket on the bed in triumph.

Just as he released the basket, her eyes fluttered open; she turned and looked up at him with a toothless grin.

"You little swindler!" he laughed, "You were faking the whole time, weren't you? This is a bad sign— I'm already rubbing off on you," he picked her up gently, bouncing her as he'd seen some other mothers do. "Your great grandma is already gone; I would bet ten to one. She's a wise old thing I must admit, but I'm glad she's gone. This place is going to be crowded enough now that you're here."

He laughed at his own joke as he left his bedroom to go out on the veranda into that sunlight, he'd dreaded only a short while before.

Gergo entered the room and quickly got things in order, after which he brought breakfast for both the people now residing on it. This was all done in record time as was usual for both Gergo and Abrax.

"Is she gone?" Abrax asked without taking his

eyes off Sancia.

"Yes, she left not long after you and I went to bed."

"Brave little thing," Abrax muttered to himself. "She's got a long journey ahead of her."

"Indeed," Gergo said, waiting for more words from Abrax. When they didn't come, he turned to go.

"Gergo, I've decided I need to go to Zacroon," Abrax said nonchalantly.

"Now?" Gergo asked, trying to conceal his surprise.

"No, not for perhaps a month or so, but there are some questions I need answers to. The old girl's story plus my brother's letter have got my mind whirling on old concerns I buried away for a later day. I'm afraid that day's come."

"What about the child?" Gergo asked.

"That all depends on how the month or so goes," Abrax answered, looking at him notably.

"Aw, so this will be a solo journey," Gergo replied let down.

"That all depends on how the month or so goes."

"What do you mean?"

"I will either be travelling alone, or I will be travelling with Sancia."

"I understand," Gergo said rather stiffly.

"Now, don't be like that, Gergo. You and I both know it will do you no good," Abrax smiled.

"If there is nothing else? I have much to do to prepare for this journey."

"No, there is nothing else but your ghastly attitude," Abrax answered, ignoring Gergo's pretext of servanthood. "Come then, give us a smile," he finished, holding Sancia up towards his scowl. She looked at him with her, now famous, toothless smile, which was now accompanied by her infectious giggle.

"Oh, that's just wonderful. . . now I have two of you to put up with," Gergo chuckled in spite of himself.

"She does have a magical kind of effect, doesn't she?" Abrax said turning her to face him.

"That's the way of babies. It's their perfect innocence which does that."

"I suppose you're right. Now, what happened to *all those things* you had to do to prepare for my journey?" he asked, furrowing his brow in ploy confusion.

"I was just going to attend to it," Gergo answered, raising his withered brow in mock dignity.

"I'm afraid you're going to have a lot to put up with," Abrax said to Sancia, at which she let out a

84

squeal of laughter.

Gergo left the room smiling at the change which had occurred almost overnight over Master Abrax. He was so much lighter since the coming of Sancia. He knew there was a great part of him grieving for the loss of his brother, a great part indeed. The child had eased the blow some.

His mind wondered at the news of this upcoming journey. There must be a *great* amount of knowledge Master Abrax is after for him to leave the home he had created to never go out in the world again. Gergo was trying to concoct what kind of disguise would best suit Abrax for this journey. He was never seen as himself except here, at his own home. Gergo was sure they would discuss this matter later.

Gergo went out into the backyard to let the dogs out. He knew they would be very rambunctious because they had been put in early yesterday. These were the famous dogs of Master Abrax, they were burly like bears with long snouts like wolves. Their fur was sleek and shiny. Most were black and a few gray. They were left in a large, long kennel that went up along some of the mountainside which included a cave where most of them slept at night.

"Alright then, brutes, out with you," Gergo

shouted as he swung open the large door.

They howled and barked in joy as they poured out across the yard, rushing towards the front yard. Abrax and Sancia watched them as they flew across the yard towards the dense forest. He smiled, feeling his defenses become heightened.

"Those, Sancia, are my dogs. . . our dogs," he corrected. "I found that breed in my travels and brough them here. There are none else like that in the entire world. They are one of the many reasons why we don't have to worry about unwanted visitors."

He spoke as she drank from a bottle Gergo had fashioned for her. She listened attentively as he spoke.

"You may ask, *Well, why weren't Grandma and I attacked when we first came?* Well, I will tell you. You see, these dogs obey my every whim because I put a certain herb in their food. This herb has a magnificent effect on this particular breed. I have been able to produce in them an allegiance to only myself. This herb intensifies this allegiance so much so, that no matter the distance, I am heard by them and I, in return, know if even a bird enters my grounds. They then wait upon my whim as to what I wish them to do. It has been one of my more successful experiments," he finished, musing over some of his much less successful ones.

"What, you don't believe me? Well, alright then. I will just have to demonstrate," he said, shrugging his shoulders as he began the demonstration.

"Come on grey," a grey dog burst from the trees, running at full speed towards the veranda on which he sat.

"You see? They are so connected in allegiance to me, it has connected their minds as a pack. They know the exact one I want and how I want that one to come. I don't have to actually say out loud my desires, I did that for your benefit. They truly are a marvelous bunch," he finished, smiling down at the large animal, which sat patiently looking up at him. He threw it a scrap off his plate and nodded a dismissal. The dog loped off back towards the woods.

"Now, let's see what Gergo has fashioned for your wardrobe. Having one of the Artur around is very handy. Especially Gergo, who is well, let's just say a very *special* one. In truth, his name is not Gergo, but that's all I will say on the matter. No, don't give me that look; I won't tell you that story until you're much older," Abrax said as he entered the room next to his, which had, as if by magic, been morphed into a splendid nursery. "I will say he and I have been allied for a few years now. He's frightfully indebted to me. I hope to get him back where he belongs one of these days.

He set Sancia in a beautiful swing, which was trimmed in white lace. It began the process of changing her flat cloth, removing the soiled one for a fresh one. He opened the closet and found, to his liking, a massive amount of frocks and frills. "Aw, yes. These will do very nicely."

He grabbed a dark purple outfit and tossed it towards the swing. Instead of falling to the floor, they zipped around the child until she was fully dressed; complete with a frilly bonnet from which some of her dark mahogany curls escaped.

"You look wonderful!" he exclaimed as he picked her up out of the superb swing. "It's time for a tour of the house. I must warn you I will not show you every room; mostly the *girly* ones, which I think you will like. Shall we start with the Flower Wing?" he asked, looking down at her expectantly. "Brilliant! You and I will get along famously if you keep this up."

Abrax smiled at his own foolishness. He thought of Achaz, and the smile dispersed. Achaz was the one who should be sharing these jokes with her. Achaz should be the one feeding her and babbling on like an idiot about nothing. He would've too.

This thought collected the smile back as Abrax pictured his brother playing with his child. He would have been far more animated and would have contorted his features until she reeled with laughter. Then he would have found anything to hide behind so he could jump out in surprise.

He would have played all the games people play with infants. He would have done it for hours after he came in from the Sea in the evening. Laughing harder than Sancia as new ideas to entertain her came to him, he would turn smiling at Jacqueline. Who would sit close by as she knitted the baby's baby clothes, perfectly pleased, along with her daughter at the wonderful man she had married.

Abrax looked at Sancia as he pictured this happy scene that would never be with the family that no longer existed here.

"I can't give you what they would have given you. I'm afraid you would have been much better off with them, but I promise you I will do the best I can."

He looked in her eyes, Achaz's eyes, "I promise you too," he finished as he looked out a large window at the blue sky above him, which very much matched the eyes of his brother, father, and now his niece. Yet, it was not the color he gazed so intently upon; it was something much more intricate.

Sancia also looked out at this sky along with him, perhaps also thinking of the parents who loved her so strongly, though for such a brief time. Her gaze remained as constant as her uncle's. They sat there in silence gazing at the sky above them in deep reverie.

"Master Abrax, were you aware Ilona was caught in the Sun an hour ago?

"Outside Redivivus," Ab stated, turning away from the window.

"Andor is not taking the loss well, it seems," Gergo answered having just received news from a Crann, who are related to the Geal, named Ebha.

"Well, one wouldn't expect him to," Abrax smirked and added, "What does Ebha say?"

"He is fuming in the Mountain, plotting revenge. She says they are plotting to flatten Redivivus tonight as they retrieve Ilona. She says they are still making no progress in reverting the Kovet Urlap you have inflicted on them."

"So they've got a nice bundle of stones building up?" he asked, smiling as he pictured Andor's frustrations. "They won't touch Redivivus. Andor knows it's too risky, however much he fumes and shakes his fists. He, as well as his followers, know the consequences of being caught in sunlight. If she had changed her loyalty, she would be herself and well. She has no one to blame but her own foolish self."

"It's a pity. . . she and I were good friends once," Gergo said mourning her loss in more ways than one.

"I'm sorry, old boy. I told you this wouldn't be easy, but it shows us that nothing has changed among our dear Artur friends."

"Yes, I know, I know," Gergo nodded his head, "It's a hard thing to know their hatred is do deeply rooted. You can't imagine what it's like to have your family hate you so."

"Yes I can," Abrax said, resting one hand on the phony aged shoulder.

"Before yesterday, I believed myself very much hated by my only family. And it would have been a hatred I earned because I refused to correct my mistake. *You did not.*"

Gergo nodded his head, feeling the comfort of these last three words soak in. Though they helped, his shoulders still sagged from the sadness.

"Would you feel better if you looked like yourself today?" Abrax asked, smiling at the immediate response.

"You mean remove this old fogey hide?" he

asked surprised. He almost had forgotten what he himself looked like under this drab Terra hoax.

"Certainly, Sancia won't tell anyone and, as long as you remain indoors, there shouldn't be a problem today."

"Now?" Gergo asked incredulously.

"As good a time as ever," smiled Abrax.

The black clothes the old servant wore began to swirl around him. Losing their shape, they moved upward just as his pool had. They quickly swirled up past his face, taking his flesh color into the swirl, and then it dispersed, leaving behind a much different figure. This man was tall, a good deal taller than Abrax. He had almost black hair and a closely trimmed beard. His eyes were a soft grey and could pierce like lightening. His build was muscular and broad, larger but similar to Abrax.

They smiled at each other while Sancia, losing interest, turned her head back to the window and the blue sky.

"I don't know, I think the old butler is growing on me," Abrax laughed.

"It feels good to be me again," he answered, breathing in deeply.

"No more Gergo?" Abrax asked.

"Bence, if you please," he grinned, taking on

his true name instead of his debased one.

"If you'd let me, I would call you that at all times,"

Abrax chided.

"No, I shouldn't let you call me it now as I am still disgraced but. . ." he didn't finish. He didn't have to.

"I was just going to show Sancia the Flower Wing," Abrax answered, changing the subject. "Would you like to accompany us, *Bence*?"

"I would. How does Sancia like her room?" he asked as they walked towards the Flower Wing.

"Very much. You out did yourself with her wardrobe," Abrax said, holding her so Bence could see his handiwork.

"The swing was my favorite part," he smiled approving. "That reminds me, what were you thinking as to your disguise for your impending journey?"

"You know, I hadn't given it much thought," Abrax said, rubbing his chin, which was rough, making him realize he'd forgotten to shave with all the excitement this morning. "I believe a fallen Solon man would suit me perfectly."

"I can't replicate a Solon!" Bence answered, shocked he would even joke about such a thing. "It can't be done and should not be attempted."

The Solon are revered by the world's peoples,

they are the oldest of the immortals.

"You won't have to replicate it, my friend," Abrax answered sadly.

"What do you mean?" Bence asked confused.

"I am a fallen Solon man, Bence," he said sighing.

Bence sat in silence as this knowledge penetrated him. So many things were beginning to make sense while others made no sense at all.

"How is that. . .possible?" he stuttered.

"Well, my father was Solon, and my mother was Solon and then they brought me into this world. . . . after Achaz, of course," Abrax smiled, knowing this was not what his friend meant.

"What about your brother's. . .?" Bence didn't finish, realizing the questions in his mind should not be anywhere but there . . . especially that one.

"Death?" Abrax finished for him and explained, "You know how, Bence. He gave his life to save another. The only way a Solon can die in this world. It was always his choice. With the last breath he drew, the choice was still there. He took the consequence of the crushing weight for the boy, so the boy could live. You see, he is *our father's son*," he softly said, quoting the words from Achaz's letter.

Bence leaned his strong frame against the wall,

so his mind could fully focus on this information without the strain of remembering to stand. It was absolutely inconceivable. He knew a dark past centered on the death of Abrax's father. But to think his brother could have his daughter lie upon his chest and still give up his life, especially for the *short* life of a Terra boy. It was hard to understand for an immortal such as himself.

"So, no disguise?" Bence asked, still dazed. He realized Master Abrax had never actually needed his services in concocting his disguises. Unlike the Artur, the Solon always have the ability to take on other people's forms, fallen or not.

"No," Abrax said, his blue eyes shining, "No disguise."

CHAPTER SEVEN

BENCE

Sancia lay asleep in her new room in a lovely little white laced crib. She enjoyed the Flower Wing and had fallen asleep in the Rose Room. Abrax sat by in a rocker, watching her gently breathe. He had always known Bence would be surprised when he found out his origin, but the extent of his shock reminded Abrax of his own shame.

He had not allowed himself to think of his father's death for a very long time. Achaz's death pricked at the old memories, and he wished more than ever they had been reunited before his death. He needed to have that portrait of them.

He was shocked to hear Achaz left everything behind at their home in Solon City, but then again not really surprised at all. Abrax had gone back to his home three years ago, in disguise of course, to find Achaz. He realized after that he probably hadn't needed a disguise, as he was changed so much from his boy self. It mattered little either way, he never would return again. There was too much there to remind him.

It never occurred to him that Achaz would also leave their home. He may not have found Achaz, but he did find answers which led to revenge—No, not revenge, Abrax chided himself, *justice.* There is a profound difference.

For not having thought about his father's death, he realized how much it consumed his life. He sat gazing at Sancia, realizing it had not done so for Achaz, who had learned to clean out the bitterness, so the heart could heal. Abrax sighed, thinking of the state of his own heart. It was still a gnarled mess from all the years of twisting and contorting it, trying to conceal the inflamed wound still festering. Would it ever truly heal? He wondered.

Sancia was a kind of soothing balm—her effect was helping the tightened muscles to relax from their

97

increasingly tense state. Oh, he was not the monster others believed him to be, but he was not the saint his brother had been. He revolted against the person he was born to be. There were definitely reasons as to why he was feared, but these reasons were made what seems a lifetime ago.

Since returning from his old home, he had been trying to make the long journey back to the road that led to the man he was raised to be, hoping there was a chance this man could still be. Perhaps it was a foolish hope but hope itself is not foolish. His thoughts turned away from this to Bence, his story, and his people.

He quietly left the room to find Bence, who he knew would be in his cave concocting some sort of wonderful thing for Abrax to enjoy. The wonder of the Artur is how far they have fallen from what they once were. They were created to create, to add beauty to this world. But to create beauty you must first have beauty within you.

They turned away from this when they discovered that they were not the only ones who could create beauty. Their greed inflamed them as they destroyed and plundered the beauty of others. Now, they could have beauty without the bother of creating it. But in doing so, they lost the actual *ability* to create.

As long as they continue on their murderous path, they can only create stupidity, Abrax mused. This is the consequence of their choice, and it is a harsh one for them.

The Artur have an incessant need for the beautiful, given to them so they would always create beauty within and without themselves. One would think they would realize their own nature, but sadly they have twisted it. They no longer desire to create beauty but to pillage it. It is often the case that the things given as our greatest blessings we contort until they become our greatest curses. Greed seeped into the heart of Bence by the counsel of Andor.

Reluctantly, Bence agreed as his greed induced him. He let Andor take a small army to one Terra village which was known for their beautiful pottery. Andor destroyed this village but did not stop there. To Bence's horror, he left a bloody trail with each footstep. When Andor returned, Bence was prepared to punish his cruelty, but then saw the mesmerizing plunder put before him. He pushed back his feelings of horror and replaced them with his lust for what lay before him and what more could be added.

Andor brought before him a striking blonde Terra woman as a gift for the King. Bence went to take her as he desired her greatly, when a handsome Terra man broke free to protect her. She was this man's *love*, his *wife*, his *greatest friend*. Andor killed this man with his already bloodied sword. The beautiful woman rushed to her sweet protector, the only man worthy of her beauty, her *love* —which is beauty at its most. Bence stared in horror at this brave man, slaughtered defending his love, who now clung to his lifeless body.

Bence no longer desired the pillaged mounds before him. They had become horrific by the innocent blood spilt to possess them. He looked to the other prisoners, allowed to live because of their fairness. What terrors had they suffered because of *his* greed?

King Bence commanded Andor to return these to their home along with all which was stolen. But it was too late. Andor and his army had tasted the lust of this perverse power and would not turn back. In losing control of himself, Bence lost control of his people.

Andor began to fight for the Throne and gained support when the others realized Bence desired to return all this beauty they had *rightfully* won. Bence was attacked by his brother and a great many of his family. The humorous thing about the whole story is Bence's capabilities are much greater than Andor ever dreamt of achieving. It would have been all too easy for Bence to crush him and his followers' woeful ways, Abrax contemplated . . . but at what cost?

The King of force Bence had been was what had led to all this brutality. He was filled with remorse for his crimes and knew his best option would be spent in finding a way to contain their greed. He caused an immediate sleep to come upon his people telling those captured to take what they could and flee. They chose to carry nothing but the body of their fallen hero. This example set before Bence taught him a lesson he would never forget.

He left his home knowing they would soon awaken. He could not stop being their King because he was long ago anointed King. They could not undo this choice, no matter what they now desired. Andor may sit on his throne, but he would never be their King. This power was and always would be outside the fool's grasp.

"Making the whole business incredibly idiotic," Abrax muttered, becoming increasingly irritated as he made his way down the stairs. It didn't say much for the Artur's sensibility to be sure.

Abrax opened the door without knocking, there was no need; Bence could sense anyone who came near his room. He entered the cave and was met with surprise.

"Well, what have we got here?" Abrax asked,

looking at an animal whose front was a massive lion with wings with the body of a large work horse. Its front feet were claws and its back feet hooves, which rested upon the pond water. It was not lifelike, as Marceline had been, because she was already living. You could see through this being.

"What do you call this. . . creature?"

"Haven't decided yet," Bence answered as he circled the creature adding more muscle here, changing the color of the mane there. "I dreamt about it last night and woke up thinking, why not?" he finished, turning towards Abrax, smirking.

"It certainly is fearsome," Abrax smiled back, "If that's what you were going for, you very much succeeded."

"I think it a pretty majestic type, don't you?" Bence asked, evaluating the animal again.

"Most definitely," agreed Abrax.

"I just worry what horror Andor will wreak with such a beast in existence," he sighed sadly.

"You can't be hindered by the bad he can do when the good you can do is so much greater."

Bence looked from the animal to Abrax and then again to the animal before him. "Once again, you are right. What else can I expect from a Solon?"

"Fallen," Abrax corrected.

"I may be a disgraced Artur, but I am still an Artur. You are not fallen but simply lost, Master Abrax."

Abrax thought about this statement quietly, considering the grave difference in Bence's disgrace and his own. He did not answer his friend because he was afraid he was certainly fallen, possibly much more than even he believed.

"Why not just create one at this point and then we will see what kind of personality is put into it?" Abrax asked thinking out loud.

"It could be a risky business as you said, it does look rather ferocious."

"Well, what of it?" he questioned. "You were an ornery ogre when I met you and look what I've done with you," he finished innocently.

"Well, I can't argue with that, but it isn't even remotely close to Sancia's accomplishment with *you*," Bence returned lightly.

"What exactly is that supposed to mean?" Abrax asked slightly tensing.

"I think you know what it means," Bence smiled humbly, "I'm glad someone can do for you what you have done for me."

I don't know that anyone can do for me what I did for you," Abrax mused, "but if there is such a person, I would put money on that little swindler," he said pleased, picturing her grin given to him this morning.

Bence nodded as he turned back to his creature and believed himself finished. "I think I will do what you say and see if this one will be accepted into life."

"Wonderful!" Abrax answered, rubbing his hands together in anticipation. "But we have to keep it a safe distance from Sancia until we see what kind of temperament it comes with. Agreed?"

"Obviously," Bence laughed.

"Why hello, ornery ogre. I thought I'd rid myself of you," Abrax shot back.

Both men smiled, knowing full well this wasn't even close to the old Bence Abrax was referring to.

"Never mind, I have to think what the name of this new animal should be," Bence said as he stood in front of the animal and looked into its eyes. "Almos," he finally said.

"Meaning?"

"The dreamt one," Bence smiled at Abrax.

"Fitting," Abrax nodded.

Bence raised one hand up to the creature's forehead and it lay down on its side. The spot where his hand touched became solid. This phenomenon spread until the animal looked like a lifeless body. Both men waited patiently. Soon, the body began to breathe and looked to be sleeping. Bence beamed, knowing it had been given its personality, its inner life force.

"Good job, old boy," Abrax said, smacking Bence on the back.

"I only create. I am not the Creator," Bence answered humbly back.

"How long before it wakes up?"

"It's hard to say. That doesn't come from without but from within."

They gazed at the beast as it slept peacefully; it looked much less fierce while in this state. Its muscles began to twitch, and it jerked its head a few times.

"Not long now," Bence said excitedly.

The animal's eyes fluttered open, and it sat up, looking at the two men before it. It then turned its gaze around the room and this new world it had entered.

"You are an almos," Bence said, bringing the beast's attention to him. It seemed to understand this and attempted to stand on its new legs. It was odd to see such a powerful animal struggle with this simplest of tasks. It finally made it to its feet and started taking a few tender steps.

"He's beautiful," Abrax said watching as the almos's mane shook with each step.

The almos walked up to Bence slowly, Bence

stood firm, waiting to see what this new event would bring. It rubbed its massive nose against Bence's chest.

"He is *much* friendlier than you were," Abrax noted.

"He is still as like a baby. It will take a few days before we know what he will become. It is important for me to be with him as much as possible, so I can try and train out his more problematic sides."

"Who would have thought we'd both have babies to bring up?" Abrax asked humorously.

"Yes well, I hope one day to bring up a baby more like Sancia than like this almos," Bence laughed.

"All in good time, Bence. The day will come again when all the Artur maiden's will be yearning for your arms."

Bence's reply to this ridiculous statement was the rolling of his striking eyes. Abrax laughed, knowing he had hit home. Bence, in his long life, had yet to marry. His former years were spent engulfed in creating and he had put off the greatest creation of all—children. He realized now just how foolish his former life had been and desired greatly to relinquish the predicament.

"Don't you have a child of your own you should be raising?" Bence asked pointedly.

"What, is my company no longer wanted?" Ab answered, ignoring his question.

Bence chuckled, "Your company is always welcome to me, as is Sancia's . . . Hopefully, she hasn't fainted from fright upstairs all alone."

"Alright, alright, I'm going. Sancia is more entertaining than you and far more accommodating," he said over his shoulder as he left the cave smirking at himself.

He liked it much better when Bence was Bence and not Gergo. But Gergo he must be for the time being. It was good to see him creating things again, especially things of such grandeur. He was the only Artur still creating as far as Abrax knew. What a great shame. So much talent wasted so they could capture the talents of others.

Tonight, Bence would once again put on his old butler frame and insist on being called Gergo. He had faltered in his duty as King, and would not rest until his people were led back from the awful path he started them on, and returned once again to their true selves. Andor was making this goal increasingly difficult.

Andor's face appeared in Abrax's mind. He was

the opposite of his brother in appearance, with his blonde hair and lanky frame; not like Bence's broad one. His features were also much sharper. The only similarity they shared was their striking grey eyes. But Andor's were a darker shade and cruelty had long emitted from them.

Abrax made his way to Sancia's room, quietly entering to see if she was still asleep. She was. He beamed in his triumph over Bence. He had been afraid Bence was right, and Sancia would be awake and upset. He sat again in the rocker so when she did awake, he would be there.

His thoughts turned to the newly arrived almos and a feeling of excitement emerged. Such a creature could do great things for him and especially for Bence. Before he could get lost in this thought, Sancia stirred and woke with a soft moan. She didn't have time to cry because Abrax had her in his arms before she could make a protest.

"I bet you are hungry. . ." Abrax said, thinking of the currently occupied Bence. "How would you like to see our kitchen?"

Sancia made no objection and off they went through the splendid mansion to find some refreshments.

CHAPTER EIGHT

JAR OF MOMENTS

Marceline sat beside Audric in Baldoin's childhood room. Each pondered quietly, lost in their own thoughts.

"You know we're not really immortal," Audric stated partially to himself.

"What do you mean?" she asked curiously.

"Well, think of what being an immortal means— first, they don't' age, but we and all other *immortals* in this world age at the same rate as mortals until our thirtieth year. We can die just as they during that time. Then our bodies are almost, but not completely, frozen in that age. If you look closely, you'll see this—I look older than Veva because she has been alive only thirty years. Second, immortals can't die, but we can."

At this point, Marceline started paying close attention to what he said next, "It takes a great deal for us to die because we are connected to this world's life, but it is possible to break that connection," he paused as he thought of this connection. "I have often envied those who are not bound as we are, such as the Terra. I saw Baldoin and his wife able to bring so many children into this world and the joy brought by each. So many of our kind cannot bear children. I, myself, have only two children; one left in this world. Imagine . . . for as long as I have lived. Losing my sweet Aimee ended even the chance of more children. Life, no matter the length or kind, offers both joys and sorrows."

Marceline sat quietly considering the words he had spoken to her. She thought of the Artur woman she saw turned to stone. Her understanding had been enlightened by her grandfather. She decided she must tell him of what she had seen of this woman and the confusion caused in her. He sat intently listening to her words, his brow furrowed in contemplation.

"You didn't hear what she cried out before the transformation?" he asked.

"No, she was a great distance from me. I only heard something about a *fiery death*."

"I have never heard of such a death before, but it was certainly inflicted upon her as some kind of punishment. That would be the only plausible explanation. You do not know the Artur as they once were. I know King Bence from the old days when we met together in the King's Counsel, with every newly anointed King. He was a very good man at that time. I remember feeling his powerful urgency to fill the new world with splendor, it inspired me with the great good I could do for my people. We *all* have changed a great deal since that time. . ."

"Andor is King now," she said forlornly, which caused Audric to burst out in laughter.

"Andor is no more King than Bibi is Queen," he finished, shaking his head.

"What do you mean?"

"All the immortal Kings were chosen by their family and anointed by our Creator at the start of this world. The only way to replace a King is to kill him, which the Artur will find very difficult—Bence is a force to be reckoned with."

"Many believe him to be dead because he has so long remained silent."

"Perhaps *so long* in Zacroon's sense, but not in mine. I am certain he lives and is working towards reclaiming his people from their sad state."

"Perhaps *he* shouldn't have gotten them into that sad state," Marceline huffed remembering the horror stories of the many villages destroyed.

"No, he should not have. . . but would you have him do to his family what I did to mine?' Audric questioned sadly, knowing he was no man to judge another.

Marceline was hit by her own double standard. No, she would not wish on anyone what had been inflicted on her. Revenge is the highest form of hypocrisy.

"Do you think she is truly dead?" she asked, her thoughts returning to the Artur woman.

"It's hard to say—it would depend on whether the connection was broken when she turned to stone. I would think it would be but only a Solon would know for sure."

"Do you know the Solon King?" she asked in wonder.

"The Solon do not have a King per se," he said smiling at the child still within the woman. "The only ruler they recognize is the Creator himself, who is, of course, King of all. They do have a man appointed to speak for them who is, in a sense their leader, but he is not their king."

Marceline took in all this new information and

felt indeed like a child who still had so much to learn.

"Is it true they live in a city in the sky?"

"It is true, and it is one of the most beautiful places I have ever seen. It used to be visible to us in the early days and shone like a beacon of hope. Now, it is all but concealed from the world. If you look closely, you will see the faint outlines of the tallest towers in the sunlight."

"Are they bound to the sky as the Mer are bound to the Sea?"

"No, they are bound to this *entire* world—they are the helpers or, I suppose, the hands of the Creator until the death of this world."

"What do they look like?"

"That is impossible to say because they rarely show themselves as themselves. The only thing they cannot change is their marvelous blue eyes, which match the sky they live in."

This information pricked at Marceline's heart, but she did not fathom why. The Solon had always fascinated Marceline. She always wished to meet one. Of course, she very well could have and not known it.

Audric and she had learned much from one another this day. She knew it was time for her to return to her home on land. There was some unfinished business to attend to before her last breath was breathed.

"I have learned so many things this day," she sighed.

"You have *done* so many things this day, you must be tired," he said compassionately.

"I am tired, my mind is tired from all the thinking it has done, but it's a gratifying kind of tired," she smiled as she gazed around her.

"Would you like to stay with us tonight?" he asked concerned.

"I would love to, but I have some things to settle on land before I pass on. I would like to return tomorrow if I am able?"

"You will always be able as long as you are alive," he answered softly as the pain of this last goodbye weighed upon him. To have her here for such a brief time was cruel, but it was a cruelty inflicted by himself, which is often the hardest to bear.

"Well, then I shall return tomorrow morning and see what other wonders you have here," she smiled as she squeezed his hand.

"I will escort you back to shore," he answered, taking her arm in his.

They walked and swam as she waved farewell to her family. She did not see Bibi, which saddened her, but she comforted herself she would see her tomorrow. The

Mer respectfully stayed behind, seeing Audric desired these moments with her.

"What does land feel like?" he asked intriguingly as they went on. Marceline smiled at the child within the man.

"It depends on what kind of land you are on. . . Dirt is soft and dry, rock is both rough and smooth, grass can be prickly and soft. Land feels like many things."

"I have often wondered what it would be like to feel sand in its dry state; the sand by the water is always muddy."

Marceline marveled how something she hardly noticed in her life was something he had longed for, for so long. They appeared out of the water and walked towards shore. She watched as her skin and hands changed again to their original state. When they reached the edge of the Sea Audric smiled as tears escaped his eyes.

"You will come back tomorrow?" he asked, taking both her hands, one of which clasped the new music box.

"The moment I awake I will come to the Sea," she answered, as happy tears escaped her own eyes in response to his tender love.

He nodded and watched her leave as the wind blew, drying his wet skin. He watched as her feet, now bare, walked upon the dry sand. To his surprise, she bent down and scooped some into her hands and walked back to him.

"Hold out your hands," she smiled as she placed the dry sand into his hands.

He breathed in almost frightened at this new turn of events. He looked to her and she nodded encouragingly. He rubbed his thumbs over this new sensation; it was rough but soft, like himself. He smiled.

"I like this," he laughed, looking up at her in delight. She joined in his merriment.

"I will bring some for you tomorrow if you will come and collect me," she said through her amusement.

"Oh yes, of course! And I will bring some of the others too. They must feel how *different* sand feels dry."

She gave him one last hug and pecked him on the cheek, just as any granddaughter would do, even if her grandfather looked to be in his thirties. He watched her go up the shore as her Zacroon neighbors ran to greet her. Many waved at the Sea King, who had before utterly terrified them. He waved back, amazed at the change in his perspective. He realized much of the goodness he had lost had been replaced. All because of the wrinkled little frame before him. He knew now, more than ever, a person's frame has little to do with who they are or what they are capable of.

Marceline turned for one last wave to her grandfather before she entered her home. He waved back and reluctantly returned to the depths of the sea. Marceline set the beautiful emerald box on the table as she retrieved a paper and pen to write a letter.

Dear Master Abrax,

Thought you'd heard the last of me, didn't you? Well, once you get past your irritation, you will be glad of what I have to say. Please don't shred this letter until you have read it fully. I come this time to share news of joy and gladness. The curse is broken, you silly boy. You need not fret over little Sancia on that account—she is now under the protection of her grandfather and mine—King Audric of the Mer. He has also agreed to be an ally to you.

I shan't go into details because I know you'd just skip over them, but I send to you the last possessions I have, which are precious to me. They are Sancia's inheritance. My cloak, which was given to Baldoin as he first came upon land and has the

power to transport a person to any place they can name. It is
important to keep the powers of this cloak as secret as possible.
Achaz's painting, which I am sure you will be glad to have, but
remember it belongs to Sancia. The last of all is a music box
which sealed the end of the curse. The beautiful voice which
sings this song is Jacqueline's. Guard each of these and they will
serve Sancia, and I suppose you, well.

The old girl,

Marceline

    She then took the portrait and the music box and wrapped the cloak around them. She took some string and tied the letter to it, so it appeared to be somewhat of a package. When she was satisfied with her work, she placed one hand on the letter being careful not to let any of her skin touch the actual cloak.

    "The Rose Room," she whispered and with that, all she had left of her former family was gone, except their memory.

    She sat at the table in silence wondering what Sancia was doing right now.

    Her thoughts whirled from her to Audric, to Jacqueline, to Abrax, to Bibi, to Achaz. It was a good thing she was sitting down, or she may have fallen over. Suddenly, a wonderful thought filled her mind. She began to search for a large old jar her husband used to fill with all kinds of buttons for her to sew onto his old coat.

She smiled at this memory and at this coat that so many odd buttons were sewn onto over the years. He had simply refused to get a new coat. It was a gift from their son, and he would practically strut around town when he wore it. She sighed as she longed to see his face once more.

She found the jar, which was now empty, as there was no coat to sew buttons onto anymore. She walked out her door and began filling the jar with sand. She smiled as she thought of the excitement this gift would bring to her family tomorrow.

This brought to her mind Audric's face as he held the dry sand in his hands. Such moments are more precious than diamonds and much more easily found.

She thought how they were like her handfuls of sand filling the jar. Each one was small but, as time went on, they filled the jar like lives are filled with moments. *A jar full of moments,* she smiled.

"What are you doin'?" a shy voice asked behind her. She turned to find Ferrelous, the boy Achaz saved, behind her, his shaggy sun-bleached blonde hair covering his hazel eyes.

"I am putting sand into this jar for my family

because they have never felt dry sand before."

"Do they not like wet sand?" he asked as he edged to her side and began helping her fill the large jar with his much smaller hands.

"Oh, I think they do, but sometimes it's nice to try new things, don't you think?"

"I don't know, sometimes tryin' new things makes bad things happen," he said this so sadly it nearly broke her heart. She knew he simply felt horrible about what happened.

"That's true, but that's when we try new things that can harm us or others around us. Do you think this dry sand will hurt my family?"

"No, I don't think so. They looked really nice today when they were huggin' you. I'm glad you're not *alone*," he said as tears filled his young eyes.

"Oh Ferrelous, you sweet little boy," she said as she took him in her arms. "I only thought I was alone. Think of it, I had that whole family right there by me all this time and I felt alone because I couldn't see them. It's the same with our loved ones who die. We can't see them, but they are always there right by us."

"Really?" he asked sniffing.

"Really," she smiled, wondering how she had ever felt anything other than the peace she felt at this moment. To blame this child for what happened would be crueler than what actually happened. "Do you remember what Jacqueline said to you before she died?"

"Uh huh," he answered as big tears rolled down his cheeks.

"I want you to remember that Ferrelous. Remember you were kept here for a purpose and knowing you as I do, I believe it is a marvelous one."

"You think I could be a great fisherman like Achaz?" he asked with hope-filled eyes.

The light cleared in Marceline's eyes. No one ever asked the poor boy *why* he had gone so far out to sea. He had been forgotten in all the chaos. The young boy had been trying to be like his hero, *Achaz.* The power of this revelation filled Marceline with great remorse. This poor boy was being weighed down far more than anyone realized.

"I think you are going to be a great *man* like Achaz," she answered, smiling down at him through her tears.

He took her words to heart as he knew she would never tell him a fib. He confidently put sand into the jar and dreamed of the day he would be the great man, like Achaz. He helped her move the jar beside her front door as it was quite heavy once filled.

"Are you going to see the Mer people again?" he asked when they set the jar down.

"Yes, tomorrow," she smiled happily. He saw how happy she was about going, and it made him happy.

"Come in for a drink, you've earned it," she said as they walked into her sparse cottage.

"Could I come and help you take the jar tomorrow down to your family?" he asked as he sipped the cool water.

"That would help me a great deal," she laughed. "I didn't realize how heavy it would be." She looked outside and realized the sunlight was fading.

"My goodness, you better get along home before your mother starts worrying."

"Alright, I'll be here early!" he answered, nodding his head up and down excitedly and then rushed out her front door. She lay down to sleep and slept until she heard a light tap on the front door.

"Come in," she called out as she slowly rose from her bed.

"I came earlier just in case I wasn't early enough," he said, seeing he was fact too early.

"You are a dear," she smiled. "Would you run and fetch your mother? You see, I think we may need more help bringing the jar down."

"Sure! I'll go wake her up," he ran off quick as a

whip.

Marceline smiled at the child as she lay back down on her bed. She would not be carrying the jar down to her family. She would not return to the Sea. She let the tears roll down her cheeks. She couldn't let little Ferrelous be here when she passed—he'd experienced enough death. She thought of Jacqueline, Achaz, her son, but her thoughts rested on her husband. She pictured his kind eyes and loving smile, which had remained constant throughout his life.

She heard Ferrelous and his mother quickly enter her home. His mother was a wise woman. She sent Ferrelous outside to make sure the jar was *still full of sand.* She knelt beside Marceline and took one of her hands.

"Thank you for what you said to Ferrelous," she said as her gratitude flowed from her.

Marceline simply nodded and gently squeezed her hand. Her breathing was labored but she was accustomed to that from the curse. She again thought of her husband and closed her eyes until her last breath left her, his face ever before her.

Ferrelous's mother kissed the old hand, which had been such a gentle might. She took the blanket and covered the sweet face. She remained on her knees beside the bed, not realizing Ferrelous had returned to report the jar was still full. His lip quivered as he left silently and returned to the jar. Tears blurred his vision as he cried on the jar. He heard a noise and looked up to see a man standing in the Sea down the shore from the house. Ferrelous knew this was her family. He straightened up and wiped away his tears. A feeling swelled within him of what he needed to do.

The jar was nearly half his size, but his determination outweighed it. His muscles ached as his small arms and legs carried the jar to the Sea King. Tears continued to fall as the boy thought of his friend, who he wouldn't see anymore. The deep sand caused him to stumble a few times, but he pushed onward. The brave boy came before the Sea King, who had nearly taken his life not so long ago.

"We can't see her anymore," he said as he set the jar down. "But she's still beside us."

Audric bowed his head and looked up at this stalwart child whom he recognized. "What is that?" he asked quietly.

"She wanted you to try somethin' new," he said as he lifted the jar to give Audric.

"Did she?" Audric smiled at the boy, who was trying to contain his emotions. He took the jar.

"Yes," the child croaked as he wiped his nose. "She said the dry sand wouldn't hurt you."

"You have been very brave and very kind," Audric said as he knelt on one knee to look into Ferrelous's eyes. "I want to give you something for what you have done for my family this day."

Ferrelous looked at him wide-eyed not knowing what to expect. He watched as Audric removed a green ring from his smallest finger. It wouldn't fit Ferrelous's largest finger, so he cupped his small hand around it as it was placed in his palm.

"When you wear this ring, you will have the ability to dwell underwater just as we do. You'll have to grow a bit before you'll be able to come but we will be waiting for you. You will always be counted as our friend and welcome in my waters whenever you desire."

Ferrelous looked down at the ring in his hand and then looked up and asked, "Do you think Achaz forgives me?"

Audric adored this child for the purity he was and the reminder of the purity he himself had once been.

"Yes," he said as he placed his hand on the small shoulder. "I am certain Achaz forgave you the moment he saw you in your little boat."

Ferrelous grasped the ring in his hand tightly, "Thank you," he whispered.

"Thank you," Audric answered as he ruffled the boy's hair. "Best be off, your mother needs you," he finished, pointing at the figure which had emerged from the house. He began to run back but stopped and ran back to Audric.

"She was really happy, you all made her really happy," Ferrelous said nodding his head empathetically.

"Thank you, Ferrelous," Audric smiled as the boy left to return to his mother.

He was grateful for these sincere words, especially as the pain of sorrow penetrated his heart. He took the jar and pressed the lid down tightly to make sure no water seeped in, and returned to meet his family who were coming to surprise Marceline with a coral gown.

CHAPTER NINE

THE SAVING BOY

Abrax sat in his library as he read Marceline's letter again. He smiled at her words to him, especially calling him a *silly boy.* Her letter intrigued him immensely. He knew she somehow had braved old Audric—no one could resist her spunk. He set the letter down and stared at the portrait, which was now placed above his fireplace. He let out a great sigh as his mind eased back into those joy-filled days.

The day this picture had been painted was one of many. He and Achaz had kept changing into ridiculous positions while the painter looked at his canvas. When he would look up to find them again moved, he would rant and rave at how he could not work with such impertinence. This led to the portrait not being a very large one, which in the end turned out to be a blessing as Achaz couldn't have carried it with him otherwise. Abrax remembered how their mother eventually came in to sit and watch them so there was no chance of further mischief.

She had found the whole situation very amusing. He forced himself not to allow his thoughts to linger long upon her because they would eventually fall upon a very different mother, one who held no such gleam in her eyes.

He had earlier played around with the cloak and found it to be an incredible gift. He wished Marceline had mentioned more as to who had given Baldoin such an impeccable gift. The only possession sent he had not examined yet was the beautiful music box.

It caused a sobering effect on him each time he held it in his hand. He gently opened the box, and the beautiful voice filled the room. He sat back in his chair with his eyes closed as he listened. When the song finished, he closed the box and thought of what a precious gift this would be for Sancia as she grew older. It was wonderful for him to hear the voice of his brother's wife.

Bence entered the room, reformed as Gergo.

He saw that Abrax was in deep thought, so he walked over to examine the portrait, curious as to what Abrax was like as a boy. He gazed at the brothers and looked at Achaz intensely.

"This is your brother?" he asked quietly.

"Yes. Handsome chap, isn't he?" Abrax said good naturedly.

"He is. He looks . . . familiar," Gergo answered bemused.

"Well, perhaps that's because he and I look a fair amount alike," he said, picking up the letter again, smirking at his compliment of himself.

"No, I know this boy," Gergo said, as realization dawned on him.

"When would you have ever met Achaz?" he asked incredulously.

"It was a few years before I met you. This boy stopped me from . . . making a drastic decision," Gergo said ashamed and began to relate the tale. "I was hiding in a Terra village disguised as a hideous . . . putrid man."

"Curious how your disguises often match your view of yourself. Your disguises are *revealing* . . . a paradox," Ab mumbled out loud. "I'm sorry continue. . ."

"Well, I was at this point a bitter frustrated

paradox. I thought for certain some of my people would remain loyal to me, but they all appeared to have fallen under Andor's flattery. I was angry but, most of all, I was very alone. It was awful, even thinking back to it makes me feel the crushing misery of loneliness. I began to lose hope and then it was lost. I began not looking for a way to regain my former life but to end my present one."

Both men remained silent as Gergo continued to think of this ghastly time in his life. He went on, "I thought I had discovered a way to accomplish this horrible choice. I left the village, which was really quiet a pleasant village, and began the journey towards my end. I came into a dense wood where I would destroy myself—The highest dishonor for any Artur, but especially for me, as their king. Yet, I then felt I was no longer an Artur, let alone a King. I felt I was no one, with nowhere I belonged. In these dense woods, I was sure I would have solitude, but I was mistaken, thankfully. This boy, a bit older, then came up to me with a friendly greeting. You can imagine the fiend I was to him."

He smiled slightly, knowing Abrax knew well the snarling Achaz would have been rebuffed with.

"He didn't even flinch, but started telling me how he'd left his home because his mother had died.

He began telling me how alone he felt because his brother had abandoned him—how he'd lost his whole family. I was about to ask him if he wanted to join me in my plans when he went on to talk of the plans for *his future.*

"He talked about finding his brother and told me, *families were created to get through life together,"* he said, quoting the boy's exact words. "He went on about having his own family someday and the importance he realized families held, now that he didn't have one. You can't believe the effect this boy had on me."

He continued as he pointed to the painted figure, "He saved my life that day. I don't know if he knew, but I believe he did. The look in his eyes seemed to say, *buck up, you'll get through this.* He didn't tell me his name; he went on his merry way in search of his brother . . . whom I found instead . . . I returned to the village, still a very bitter, frustrated paradox, but I no longer felt alone. I knew somewhere out there was a boy who lost just as much as I and still hoped onward," Gergo shook his head at the amazing circumstances.

Abrax sat in contemplation, thinking of this young Achaz who must have suffered so much. "Achaz always knew how to get through to buck people up," he said, knowing the truth in his words. "He did so for me unknowingly all these years we've been separated. I'm glad he found you, I only wish he had found me."

"Perhaps if he did, he never would have made it to Zacroon and met Jacqueline," Gergo said reflecting. "We've all made and not made decisions that have changed our course. You will never know what would have happened if he had found you, but I know what would have happened *if he hadn't found me . . .* I suppose this puts me more in your debt than ever."

"No. It puts us both more in Achaz's debt. The only sparks of Solon left in me are because of him. What I did for you was part of that and also part of my own selfish interest."

"No matter the reason, you helped me come out of my bitterness and anger so I could actually do something for my people. You picked up where your brother left off. The work between the two of you was the completion of saving my life, "Gergo humbly spoke.

Abrax sat quietly thinking over this story of his brother, and felt the stab of sorrow come as he once again remembered he was gone.

"You have given me much to think over," Abrax said as he prepared to retire for the night, knowing he would not be sleeping anytime soon, "Oh, by the way, how is the almos doing?"

"Extremely well. He's a very loyal creature."

"Good, I'm glad. That is especially important in any sort of companion," Abrax remarked as he thought of the friendship he held with this man; well, the man beneath this man. "I believe I'm going to make that trip sooner than I expected since we have Marceline's lovely cloak."

"Will you be taking Sancia or leaving her behind?"

"I will leave her. I don't plan to be gone long or stay the night now that I have the option to bounce back and forth as I please," he finished happily at the thought.

"What are you after?" Gergo asked hesitantly, knowing he was letting his curiosity get the best of him.

"Knowledge, truth, wisdom. . . What is any Solon after?" Ab smiled as he left the room and called back, "Good night!"

Gergo remained and stared at the face of the young, Achaz. He finally knew the identity of the saving boy. How many times he had sent a prayer of thanks for this boy, he could not count. He turned away as the emotion began to overtake him, thinking of his gratitude for these brothers who stood side by side.

133

He wondered if Achaz was sent to save him by the Solon. *No,* the answer came to him softly. He was guided by the Creator and listened to the call; even after all he had passed through.

A feeling of both intense shame and gratitude filled him. Bence had been willing to abandon the power and responsibility given to him by this same Creator; willing to turn his back on his family and leave them in the hands of Andor. How grateful he was for Achaz, who was not only willing but *did* live up to his own power and responsibility. Achaz was abandoned and yet, never stopped searching for his broken brother.

He saw Marceline's gifts on the table. The beauty of the music box drew him to it. He picked it up and examined the intricate designs of the silver in emerald. He had very little experience with this kind of beauty, the beauty of the Mer. If was gracefully subtle and deliciously refined. He liked it very much. He opened it to discover what sublime contests it contained and was startled when it began to sing.

He regained himself as he heard the mellifluous voice ring out. He unconsciously let out a sigh and sat down in the chair Master Ab formerly sat in. When the song finished, he closed the music box and opened it again to hear the song one more time. He grinned at his own foolishness.

He left the things in the library, knowing Master Abrax would study them further later. He entered the cave and was met by the almos. He desired to create a female one but knew he mustn't be hasty. This almos was still very young and needed more time to show its full character.

"Hello, boy," he said as he patted its head. He had made sure to transform in front of the animal to avoid any unnecessary confusion.

He knew the Geal would be here soon to light many of Asulon's rooms and, of course, the glasshouse. He thought of their dutiful service to Abrax and now realized why they were so fervent. They have a great love for the Solon and are one of the only other peoples who can freely enter their city in the sky. Of course, they would recognize him as a Solon. Not to mention, Master Abrax's protection of their own little city from the Artur, who would very much wish to have them for their own egocentric purposes.

He walked to the back door and opened it as he heard them jabbering about the *Mer guest* and hoping that, maybe for some reason, she had been able to stay.

"Hello, my friends," he said smiling.

"Hello! Hi! Good evening!" they all shouted simultaneously.

"How was the flight down? Any sign of trouble tonight?

"No, they are all preoccupied with retrieving Ilona and have backed down from attacking Redivivus. Of course, we all knew they would," Finn answered confidently, turning to the others.

"We did. Just so. From the start," they chirped.

"I thought so too, but they are becoming more aggressive, aren't they?" Gergo asked for affirmation.

"It's true. Andor is determined to unravel the Kovet Urlap and then conquer everything remotely in his grasp," Finn answered knowing how ferocious they were in the moonlight. "You should hear the promise he's made about what he is going to do to Master Abrax and well. . . you."

"Don't worry, my friends. I've yet to see any outsmart Master Abrax."

"He does always seem to be one step ahead of the rest of us, doesn't he?" Finn smiled to the others knowingly.

Gergo smirked knowing what they were knowingly smiling about. He didn't see a reason to tell them he knew Master Abrax was a Solon. "Well, the night grows on. Best be off. I'll see you back here for report."

"Yes, yes, can't just hang around with our jaws

flapping!" Finn said as they whizzed off speedily.

Gergo heard the others echoing, "Jibber jabber. Lip smacking. Tongue wagging."

He laughed as he returned to his room, feeling a deep appreciation for the time he was able to spend with the wonderful Geal. They had always been friends to the Artur as they both inhabited the mountains. Sadly, this friendship was dissolved with the current Artur. He was the last hope of retaining the ancient bond.

He gazed at his reflection in a tall mirror—His sad grey eyes stared back at him. Such a wonderful thing it was to be himself even for a brief time. He turned away pained from his current situation. What he needed was a little rest before Finn and the others came back. The emotional strain of the day, especially the discovery of Achaz, had taken its toll.

He thought of Abrax's words on how his disguises always matched his view of himself. It was too true. He did think of himself as an old, tired man. The almos lay asleep, softly breathing, at the foot of his bed. He eased his haggard body down onto his bed and told himself what time to arise again. Immediately he was asleep and resting his outwardly withered frame.

The almos stood suddenly as if patiently waiting for this moment to arise. He walked over calmly to the side of the wrinkled body. The massive animal sat there staring at him with a meditative look. He leaned his large head down closer to the smaller sleeping one.

"I won't fail you," he whispered in a deep, strong voice. He then returned to the foot of the bed and lay down as though he were sleeping. Who could say if he truly was. . .

CHAPTER TEN

ROOM OF KNOWLEDGE

Ab awoke excited for his journey, wondering what Marceline would think when she saw him. He had to admit he wasn't dreading seeing the wrinkled face again. He had formulated various questions to which he needed answers. But above all he needed to get inside Achaz's cottage. He knew there would be records and journals hidden somewhere in it—Achaz's life work. All Solon keep such records for themselves and for their posterity to learn from. He knew Marceline didn't know anything about them which made him wonder as to how much he would find.

He and Sancia ate a quick breakfast. He knew she would fall asleep soon because she had hardly slept at all the previous night.

He couldn't understand what all the fuss had been about. The bassinet Gergo made for her was much better than the basket bed he concocted.

Perhaps she wasn't used to sleeping alone yet? But she slept fine alone during the day. He looked at his reflection and saw the drowsy face staring back at him. If he wasn't so excited about what he would find in Zacroon he probably would have taken a nap along with her.

When the little beauty was sleeping, he hurried to the library for the cloak. Gergo was busy observing and teaching the almos. He had earlier informed Abrax he had decided it was time for him to give it a pet name but wished Abrax's input on the matter. This would all have to wait until he returned.

He wrapped the cloak around his shoulders which somehow transformed into the right length and was no longer faded, as it had been with Marceline. *New owner, new life,* he speculated. He wondered if the cloak aged along with its wearer and that's why it had faded, perhaps causing it to be less effective. He sat for a moment staring at Achaz's young face in the portrait and let out a long breath of anticipation.

"Achaz's cottage in Zacroon," he said loudly, hoping this cloak could handle the long distance.

Before he realized it, he was standing in a quaint little room. The sun was barely rising so the room was not yet well lit. Abrax observed that it hardly had anything left in it except some furniture. Yet, he could still feel the warmth of the place. He could almost see Achaz sitting at the table, discussing all sorts of subjects with Jacqueline as they breakfasted together. He turned away from the vision knowing if he persisted, he would lose his composure. Many of the greatest pains occur in thoughts.

He assessed the cottage and saw numerous places for hiding the sacred goods he sought. He searched through these but came up empty-handed. Dropping down beside the table, he grew frustrated with Achaz and his thoroughness. Of course, he shouldn't have expected anything less. He strummed his fingers on the table as he looked over the walls and floor again for any other options.

It was at this moment his eye caught on the wood ceiling made of beams with gnarled knots. In the hole of each knot were placed various colors of glass-like pebbles angled towards the window. The sunlight was starting to shine into the room and reflecting off these pebbles, filling the drab room with the colors of life. His eyes moved from these many knots until they fell on a very small one, much smaller than the others. Shaped in the form of an eye, it contained a sky-blue pebble as its iris.

Ab smiled gleefully. Only a Solon would find significance in this knot and only Ab would know what that significance was. Achaz had prepared and hoped Ab would come and use his life's work if disaster struck. Their father had used this very symbol to hide his own life's work.

Ab walked over to the knot and pushed the pebble in with his finger. The pebble began to emit a great amount of blue light until a blue ladder appeared before Ab. Where the eye had been was now a bright hole for him to climb into.

Ab did climb and found himself in a very different scene from the cottage below. This massive room was filled with an assortment of things from leather bound books to brush-stroked paintings. He saw one of these paintings was Achaz as a man with what must be Jacqueline on their wedding day.

There were shelves of books full of Achaz's wisdom and experiences. The room itself was indeed large and appeared to have an open roof, allowing the bright sky to enter from above. The walls were a pale blue with emerald designs swirling throughout. Musical instruments, he soon discovered, as they dabbed the view before him, many of which Abrax was unfamiliar with.

This room was the marriage and life of Achaz and Jacqueline. He saw two desks which sat facing one another in the center of the room. One was bulky, made of a light glazed wood with many knots and covered with papers—it had a portrait of Jacqueline on it. The other was made of a dark, sleek shiny wood with lovely carvings on the legs and sides. It held many odd assortments, one of which included a strange instrument clearly still in the process of being painted. It had a portrait of Achaz on it.

He walked over to Achaz's desk and saw an opened book upon it. He sat down in his chair and noticed the date was in the year their mother had died. He read:

Today is a day I can't and won't forget. My mother passed away. As you know, we can't die unless we give our life for another's. My mother gave her life for her sons by giving it for a baby bird which had been knocked out of its nest. Just as Ab, her baby, had been knocked out of our nest. You may see this as untrue or a sorry loss of life, but if you read further, you will see it was really a gift from the Creator.

I had hoped she would come back to me but she never did. When I spoke to her, she just stared at me vacantly, almost like she was locked inside herself. She couldn't bear to live separated from my father until the death of this world —who knows

143

how long that will be.

She didn't give her life for that bird; she gave her life for me and Abrax. The bird was just the means to an end. She knew deep down Ab was somewhere in the lower lands and I couldn't find Ab while I was taking care of her. So she gave her life for her own baby bird because she couldn't regain her life here. I know she tried hard to do so. I could see it in her eyes, like she was in this constant battle to get control of her mind again. She was Solon Strong to the end. I was with her as she passed. She smiled just like she did before all this. I know she is happy now with my father.

I must go and find Ab. I feel so alone here in our home with no one but me here, it's not home anymore. There is nothing here I want or need more than him back in my life. I have missed him horribly through all this. I still can't believe he's out there somewhere alone and broken. I'm frightened to leave my home, but I'm more frightened I'll never see Ab again. I miss him, I miss my father, and I miss my mother. I can't write anymore now, it's just too hard.

I'll write again soon, hopefully with happier things to write about.

Achaz

Abrax wiped his wetted cheeks as he cursed his wretched self. Why had he left Achaz to carry on alone?

144

Why had he been so weak? Achaz was forced to carry it *all,* completely alone. Ab mourned his mother's heartrending death. He realized how much he was like her. How the severity of his father's death impacted them both into extreme reactions. It was poignant thinking of her in such a suffering state. It's different for immortals to lose a loved one. They must wait a great deal longer to be reunited than mortals.

But Abrax knew this was not the reason behind his mother's death. Achaz was right. She had died for them. She always put them first. This was at her core and nothing, not even the loss of her mind, could change that. When she realized she couldn't come back, she let go, with steady Achaz by her side.

"I'm so sorry, brother," Ab whispered hoarsely as he gazed around the room in which he sat.

The way things were left made it feel as if at any moment, Achaz and Jacqueline would enter the room together laughing about some moment they just shared. Ab stared around in reverence, glad his brother found someone he could depend on. He more than deserved such a someone.

Ab realized he would need Gergo, no Bence, after all. He could not have dreamed Achaz would have accomplished all this by the way Marceline described his life. Of course, again, he should not have been surprised. He gazed at the many paintings, trying to pull his mind out of his sadness. He found one that must have been the most recent. It was of Achaz, Jacqueline, and Sancia looking healthy and happy. Ab realized this to be the last work Jacqueline's anguished hand painted before she died.

He noticed Jacqueline's beauty was similar yet different from her grandmother. She bore the same creamy skin and striking eyes, but her eyes were larger and more dazzling. Her figure was more womanly than her grandmother's and her hair a deep auburn, which set her eyes and skin off perfectly.

He looked at Achaz the man, grown broad and probably slightly taller than Abrax. He epitomized those rugged good looks women adore with his dark brown hair, a few shades darker than Ab's, and his strong jaw line. Ab could still see the boy he had known within the manly features. The eyes were the same, the smile was the same, the personality emitted from this portrait and the portrait Ab had was similar. Perhaps with a little more dignity in his manly countenance, but the mischievous boy was still present, Ab grinned.

He turned away realizing he needed to find Marceline and begin the process of purchasing this cottage. He needed to begin setting up barriers and defenses. He went to the only door in the room and opened it. This led him back into the former cottage kitchen. The door disappeared after he closed it. He smiled at Achaz's whimsical ways.

He entered the streets of Zacroon and saw a large crowd gathered around the cottage next door.

A sense of dread filled him, and he felt the urge to walk the other way. Shaking this off, he joined the increasing crowd of Terra.

"What's the trouble?" he asked a middle-aged man beside him.

"Old Marceline passed away," the man said sadly not taking his gaze from the cottage door. "Alura was with her when she died, thank goodness."

Ab sat there in stunned silence. Trying to process the man's words. *Gone.* He noticed a small boy standing by the door weeping.

"Who is that?" he asked his informer.

"That's Ferrelous, Alura's son. He was here when she died too, poor boy," the man answered, still taking no notice of the stranger asking him questions.

Ferrelous. The name struck as he looked at the boy for whom his brother's life was given. Ab could not discern the child clearly as he was at the back of the crowd, but he very much desired a closer look. Even from a distance he could see there was something . . . *peculiar* about this Ferrelous. It would have to wait.

He left the crowd and the deceased behind him as his mind turned over new options. Returning to the Room of Knowledge, he took three books dated for the younger years, when the family was together in bright days and pleasant nights, before misery thrashed its despondent whip. These would be a happy read.

"Asulon Mansion, Library," he said with the books grasped tightly in his arms. He was again in his library and let out a deep sigh. He went over and pulled the crimson rope.

Gergo entered the room almost immediately and full of animation. This caused Abrax to be unable to get a word in because Gergo entered with words out.

"He can talk!" Gergo said trembling from excitement.

"Who can talk?" Ab asked bewildered.

"The almos! My creation was instilled with a talking life force! He has an intelligent mind," Gergo blabbered.

"Ability to talk doesn't always imply intelligence," Abrax smirked. "That is very intriguing news, my friend."

"I should say so, Master! I have never, not in all

my days, created something given a talking life force,"
Gergo rubbed his hands together eagerly. "But you rang
for me so you must have news from your own journey,"
he finished, turning attentively to Abrax.

Abrax sat in silence for a moment, not wanting to
take away from his friend's moment of joy.

"How is Sancia?" Ab asked.

"She ate a little more and then conked off again.
You would think she had Artur in her the way she can
fall asleep so fast," he laughed.

"Perhaps you are rubbing off on her," Ab smiled
slightly. Silence followed as Gergo awaited the news
which he noticed Master Ab was reluctant to give.

"What is it?" he asked.

"Marceline died early this morning, I saw the
young boy my brother saved, but that is not the half of it.
I found my brother's Room of Knowledge and it is
enormous—full of Achaz and his wife's life work. I can't
begin to tell you how much there is. I brought the first
three books of his life work with me. He began when he
was nine. Remarkable, isn't it? He must have gone back
to our home and retrieved them after he left. . ." Ab
finished, realizing this point and wondering when Achaz
returned.

Could it have been around the same time Abrax
had? He didn't tell Gergo about his mother, nor would

he. It was too painful and the shame he felt for his past was already full.

"Do you think it could be transported here?" Gergo asked. "Perhaps with your help we could do it. . . but the Solon power is so remarkably complex. It would take a great deal of time—if it is even possible.

"I'm not sure. The room itself is massive and seems to be interwoven into the cottage itself. A great part of me thinks Achaz meant it to be by the Sea and designed it to be unmovable. It would make perfect sense—it's where they lived and loved one another. I feel he would find it insulting if we attempted to move it. After seeing it, I doubt we could attain it, my brother was a very prudent man. No, my goal and current worry is securing the cottage it's connected to, so Sancia will always have access to it. No one but family can enter a person's Room of Knowledge, but anyone could enter the cottage and that simply will not do."

"I'm sure that can be accomplished without much fuss," Gergo smiled.

"It'd mean a great deal, Bence," Ab answered waiting for the correction.

Gergo let it slide this time.

CHAPTER ELEVEN

FOURTEEN YEARS LATER…

Sancia sat at her mother's desk in her parents' Room of Knowledge scrutinizing her painting. It was a present for Uncle Ab, a portrait of her and him as their current selves. She sighed as she gazed at her last painting, which was still drying, a portrait of her parents and herself. It was going to be placed next to the last portrait her mother painted, which included her as an infant.

She was fourteen years old now. Her mahogany hair was thick and long with a gentle wave. Her eyes were large as her mother's and blue as her father's. She was growing into an angelic beauty.

She was a talented painter like her mother, but

not quite at her mother's level of perfection. She loved this room more than any other place in the world. More than the Sea, more than the Rose Room, even more than Uncle Ab's library.

She had gone to the Sea earlier to visit Grandpa Audric but had spent most of her time with Bibi until Ferrelous came. It was so *obnoxious* how he and Bibi were together. Bibi was three years older than Sancia and Ferrelous was nearly one year older than Bibi.

He thought he was so mature because he would be turning eighteen soon. Sancia and Bibi were best friends and had been for as long as she could remember. Grandpa Audric adored them both but Sancia somewhat more. Bibi could be rather silly sometimes, especially when Ferrelous was around.

Sancia set her paintbrush down and walked over to her father's desk, which had an open book on it. She sat down and began reading his words, written when he was her age. He had had much larger worries than puppy love. She read:

Today my father was murdered by a Volos man. I can barely write through my tears, but I can't express what I am feeling in any other way. Mother is broken. I've never seen her like this before. She's always been so cheerful, but all that seems to have been sucked out of her. All that is left is this hollow void. I snuck to overhear what Alder was saying to her. It was his son's life that was saved by my father, at least I think he said it was his son. But I don't know how it could be possible. Alder is a pretty old man to have a baby and his wife left him a long time ago. The child is a mystery. It seems Alder had been somehow tricked by a Volos man into some kind of debt. This killer was demanding Alder's child's life for payment. How this is a form of payment I can't understand. Alder came to father for help, seeing no other way out.

I never heard him say exactly what his debt was. What I gathered to have happened was the Volos man gave Alder a gift of some sort and then wanted it back, saying it wasn't a gift at all. Only the gift had somehow disappeared. Seems to me it was just another sick Volos trick. Father, of course, being father, stepped in.

I know he was right but a part of me wishes he hadn't. That's my weakness, though. I am proud to be his son and hope one day I can be a man like him. I will keep him in my mind constantly, so I will always be taking steps toward becoming like him. I summed up from what Alder said that his child was somehow special. He talked of him almost as though he wasn't Terra at all. It was all spoken in hushed tones, and mother already seemed to understand. It was almost as though father had been on some kind of mission to protect him.

It's sad but I really don't care about any of this. I just want my father back. His death keeps flashing through my mind no matter how much I try to fight it. Poor Ab can't stop trembling. I don't want to write this part down but I feel I must. I am no longer the boy I was before. The Volos man whose name I don't know took the form of a black panther- Volos are shapeshifters, or I guess you could say adapters. This man chose this form to end another's life. He was more an animal than a man, no matter what appearance he wore. Alder had come earlier with the baby to our home for protection. A very big deal for a Terra. The Volos came into our yard. How he was able to enter our city, I don't know. Someone must have given him entrance. Who among our kind would do such a thing? My brother and I were hiding from mother, who was trying to teach us baking techniques.

I wish more than anything we had been in the kitchen with her instead of behind the rose bushes in the front yard. Father met the beast with his steady walk. I was sure he would take the thing by the tail and send it packing, until the animal struck and father didn't so much as raise one hand to shield his face. He just took the blows. Ab clung to me so tightly, it was difficult for me to rise. I don't know what I was thinking I could do. I just had to do something.

I rose and was about to rush the animal when I felt my mother's hand grab my collar. She pulled me and then Ab through the window as my father was taking his last breaths. I was so angry, I ran while she pulled Ab in. I heard her yell behind me but I couldn't sit by. I am not a child anymore. I am almost a man and a man doesn't hide behind his mother.

I ran past Alder, who was sobbing holding the baby. I didn't care a heap for his tears. The panther ran when I burst from the doorway. "Coward!" I shouted after him over and over again. "Meet me as a man, you coward!" When I reached

154

father, he was almost gone. His face was scratched up but not too bad. I won't describe his fatal wounds because I'm already crying.

I took his hand in mine and just sobbed like the child I just said I wasn't. He opened his eyes; one was swelled some but I could see his blue eyes staring up at me. They filled with tears and he tried to raise his arm to ruffle my hair like he always did but he couldn't lift it. I just cried on him like a little girl. He squeezed my hand that held his and nodded at me. He was saying, "Be strong son, be Solon Strong."

When mother and Ab were running up, he heard them and nodded to me again. "Take care of them." He was gone before they reached us. I told them he knew they were coming for him and smiled in his passing. I can't speak of this ever again. I don't know if I will ever write of this again. I feel as though I have all those gashes on my father's body, only you can't see mine. I wish I had been at his side through every blow given him. I wish I had been next to mother holding her in her agony. I wish I wouldn't have left Ab behind.

I'm glad I was there with him before he passed. He may have been alone in the battle but not in the victory. You may wonder at me calling this a victory but for the Solon, saving a life is always a victory, even if it costs you your own. Alder will raise this child to whatever purposes he was meant. Just as my father raised me to be the man I was meant to be. I am a man from this day forward. I will be a man like my father and I hope that, if one day I am put in his situation, I will know what the right choice is and *brave it just as he.*

I am so thankful for Ab. Mother has not spoken since being at the side of father's dead body. Our kind learns of the possibility of death but don't exactly expect it. She is the shell of who she once was. Alder tries to console her, but even he, as her and father's dear friend, can't get through. She doesn't blame him or the child, I can tell. She just can't seem to bare this world without father in it. Ab and I will pull her through. Together we can accomplish anything. Ab is as smart as they come and I know we'll get through this together.

Achaz

Sancia's tears wetted the page as her father's when he had written it. She sat still trying to regain control of her emotions. She was so proud to be his daughter. He was so brave even then. She missed him and her mother even though she didn't remember her time with them. This room connected her to them. She was thankful to them and also Uncle Ab, who'd taken her in.

Her thoughts turned to this baby boy that was saved by her grandfather Amon, how her father thought he wasn't a Terra, and how there might be something special about him. She wondered if this was the same case for Ferrelous. She discerned Uncle Ab knew something about him but, for the life of her, he wouldn't spill it. Well, perhaps for the life of her, but nothing short of it.

He just insisted she keep reading her father's records. He had read them many times and never tired of his brother's wise words. She sighed, realizing it was about time she should return to Asulon Mansion. She walked over to a navy-blue love seat upon which her cloak was resting. It matched the love seat in color and obtained a hood in her ownership of it. She wrapped it around her and said lazily, "Asulon." She didn't have to be specific; she and the cloak had acquired a kind of unity.

"Hi, Gergo," Sancia spurted, appearing in the library. Gergo started at her in surprise. She giggled at this as it was one of her favorite accomplishments. It was very hard to catch Gergo off guard.

"Don't you *Hi* me! How did you know I'd be in here?" he laughed.

"Lucky guess," she smiled. She had a lot of those.

"Master Ab, is expecting you in the Silver Dining Hall," he answered, grabbing a handful of books he desired to read this evening.

"Alright," she said, disappearing from the library and reappearing in the Dining Hall.

"Did you scare him?" Uncle Ab smiled.

"How did you know?" she asked surprised.

157

"Lucky guess," he smirked. She stared at him, wondering how he always seemed to know everything. She wondered if her father would have been the same way. *Of course, he would have,* she thought smiling.

"How is Audric doing?" he asked, as he took a bite of food. He had clearly begun his meal before she'd arrived.

"You started without me? How rude!" she answered in mock offense, not surprised at all, as this was a common occurrence.

"My stomach persuaded me," he smiled and then awaited her response to his former question while she found her place beside him.

"He is a pearl, just as usual. He is so sweet, it's hard to believe the stories about him and all my other family. . ." she finished musing.

"Did you ask him about his wife Aimee yet?" he asked, already knowing the answer.

"No, I chickened out again. . . I got side tracked by Bibi and all her nonsense about Ferrelous."

"Are they still at that old game?" he asked, really not caring but knowing she did.

"Yes, and it is almost nauseating. Actually, it is just plain nauseating."

"It won't last," Abrax said knowingly.

"How would you know that?" Sancia inquired laughing, not putting it past him to actually know.

"Puppy love is one of the easiest things to predict, my dear," he slightly smirked, knowing Bibi was indeed beautiful but, all in all, a very silly girl and probably would remain so in womanhood. That was no match for Ferrelous, no match indeed.

"I read about *that day*. . . you know, when my father was my age," she said, changing her tone drastically.

Abrax slowly breathed in. He had tried to prepare himself for this moment.

"What did you discover about your father?" he asked. "He was very brave. . . I feel so inadequate as their daughter," Sancia whispered sadly. "I feel like I'm expected to be like them, and I just don't think I can ever be *that* good."

Abrax sat thinking about how he himself felt the same about his own parents and brother. He thought of how good Sancia already was at her young age, far exceeding himself at her age. She was amazing in her quest of becoming.

"Well, do you ever want to be *that* good?" he asked.

"Of course I do!" she said surprised at this question.

"Then you can be *that* good and, more importantly, you will be *that* good," he said pointedly. "All you have to do is *keep them in your mind constantly, so you will always be taking steps toward becoming like them,*" he spoke as he watched her eyes take on the realization. Achaz had become who he was because of who he had been trying to become. "All of us should try to be as those most like the Creator,"

Sancia sat taking this in. She knew Uncle Ab had not always done this because he'd told her so. He was an exceptionally different person than the person who had met her great grandmother Marceline. True, he still hardly left his home, but he was much gentler and, especially, more kind. Had Sancia's presence turned this place into a home, or had he turned this place into a home for Sancia? Whichever the case, the change revolved around her, or so he told her.

"I'm glad I have you," she smiled taking his hand.

This action caused his heart to swell with joy and he smiled, pushing his emotions down. "I'm glad I have you too."

"Is that why you didn't send me to a boarding school?" she teased.

"One of the many reasons," he smiled back, as Marceline's words echoed in his mind, "*This is not our home—it is just our boarding school.*"

"We should play games with Gergo in the library tonight," Sancia laughed as excitement burst from her eyes, thinking of Uncle Ab's and Gergo's jibs at one another. She loved them both dearly. Abrax agreed to this idea. Gergo needed such distractions a great deal.

He had not been Bence since Sancia was a baby, as Abrax felt it was best. The Artur were growing in the wrong direction and the time was soon coming when drastic actions would need to be taken. Gergo would have to be Bence and Bence would have to be King. Sanca was growing more beautiful by the minute and would soon blossom into womanhood. This impending gloom weighed upon Ab's mind as he and Sancia made their way to the library to play some games.

CHAPTER TWELVE

SOLID FOUNDATION

Ferrelous sat outside his cottage home in a honeysuckled state, his long legs outstretched. Bibi was so beautiful and captivating. It was so unjust she couldn't leave the Sea to be with him more often. His mother, however, was perfectly pleased with this fact. He had made the mistake of introducing them a few days ago.

It was much too soon and neither of the two ladies was ready for it. He'd concluded this was the reason as to why the outcome had been so rough. Bibi was no lover of the land and said some unkind comments about Zacroon. He couldn't blame her though; it was rather bleak compared to where she lived.

Why, hadn't he worked on his manner of speaking to be more eloquent than his fellow fishermen? He was well aware of where Bibi came from and couldn't blame her for her behavior. However, his mother felt no such sentiments of compassion.

He thought of how this emotion matched those of Sancia for him—she had been so agitated when he showed up. He smiled at this thought. She was just too immature to understand love. One day, she would and then, he would tease her about how she'd made such a fuss over Bibi and him.

"How did you fare today, dear?" Alura asked, smiling at her son's distant gaze. His hair was still that streaked and striking blonde against his tanned skin. He'd grown tall and was in the process of filling into his heightened stature.

"Pretty good. I think I'm on my way to being as good a fisherman as Achaz was," he answered proudly.

"I see. . ." she mused. "And are you on your way to bein' as good a man as Achaz was?"

This rebuke hit its mark. He knew he had a long way to go in that respect. It was a good thing he had her around to keep him focused on what was really important. Sometimes, he was still such a child.

"Trying to be, mom; trying to be," he said, hugging her. It takes a strong woman to be a mother, and a steady woman to be a good one.

"Come in and have some soup; that is, if you can still stand the company of a mere *Terra*," she said smiling at him teasingly.

"Bibi means well. She just isn't used to anything but the Sea."

"My boy, I'm not used to anythin' but the land; that don't give me a right to turn up my nose at others who aren't."

Ferrelous thought about this statement and realized its truth, but he also knew that Bibi was young and that added to her inexperience. Alura smiled as she saw the working mind of her son trying to come up with some new excuse for the girl. Eventually, those excuses would run out and all he'd be left with is the simple truth. She hoped this would be sooner rather than later.

"Sancia stopped by today," she said changing the subject.

"Did she?" he asked, not surprised.

"You know it never ceases to amaze me how thoughtful that girl is. She is so mature," she said as she scooped some soup into their bowls.

"Well, she may be thoughtful but that doesn't mean she's mature," he said, going back to his former thoughts of her lack of love knowledge.

"Bein' thoughtful is the sign of true maturity, Ferrelous. Don't you forget that — in life or in love."

He sat there, thinking again of his mother's wise words. He supposed Sancia might be more irritated about how he and Bibi practically ignored her when they were together. It was quite difficult not to, though, because they were so caught up in their love for each other. Mom just didn't understand, Mer love is different.

"Mer don't love that way," he said matter-of-factly.

"Fiddlesticks. You mean Bibi don't love that way. You think good and hard as to why her *love* isn't thoughtful. I'll be ready and waitin' to discuss it with you then."

He sat in irritated silence, partly because she was *still* treating him like a child, but mostly because he knew she was right. He focused on the former because it made him feel like a man, while the latter made him feel like a child. She sat eating her food, trying to hide the smirk making its way to her lips.

Her thoughts turned to her husband and how

165

he also would have enjoyed this exchange as much as she was enjoying it. What a pity he was in the neighboring village for market.

Raising Ferrelous brought them both much joy these many years. It was a simple, good life. She knew Ferrelous was destined for more, but this solid foundation would keep him from tumbling down when that destiny came. This reminded her the time was soon coming for him to be made aware of his future. His eighteenth birthday had always been one she felt to be forever away. Now it was practically knocking at the door.

"When does father get home?" Ferrelous asked politely, still offended at her treatment of him.

"I would think in an hour or two," she smiled, knowing he knew full well what time his father regularly got home from market.

"Well, I'm going to take a walk then," he stated formally.

"What a great idea. You have a lot of *thinkin'* to do," she replied, no longer able to contain the smirk as she began to wash the dishes.

He looked at her remarkably irritated as he plopped his dishes in the soapy water with a splash. At this, a chortle escaped her mouth. He looked at her in disbelief. How *immature,* he thought. He abruptly left the house, shutting the door loudly so she could not mistake his displeasure.

He walked quickly, without really thinking of his path, which, soon enough, led him to the doorstep of Marceline's old cottage. It had been bought by Sancia's uncle and left vacant, but it remained well kept. He sat down and leaned his back against the familiar wood. It was almost as if the memories of the place caused his vision to clear as his thoughts turned to his mom's words and actions.

More importantly, his mind turned towards his own words and his own actions. He began to smile, which soon turned into a chuckle. He could almost feel Marceline there beside him, shaking her head at this still very young and foolish kid. He thought of Bibi and how she was really very careless about. . . well, everything. Comparing her to Sancia, he saw that of the two, Sancia was much more gentle and she was only a *child*.

He sighed as he pushed his hands beneath the cool sand. He thought of Marceline and the impact the last day he'd spent with her had on him. True, he was rather young at the time, but he still remembered filling the jar with this sand. It seemed very important at the time, almost as important as carrying the jar to Audric. He knew that act was why Audric allowed him to be so attentive with Bibi.

He looked at the green ring on his smallest finger. This brought a smile to his face. He remembered all those years of yearning for this ring to fit this finger just as it had Audric's. Somehow, he had thought it would be a sign he'd obtained manhood. As if the size of a finger had anything to do with being a man. He thought back on those years of his life. It all seemed so leisurely when he was younger; now it was becoming fully fleeting as he grew older.

His thoughts returned once again to Bibi. There was nothing to be done. He realized he would have to break things off with her. It was a nice episode while it lasted, but looking back, he realized how often he was perhaps not annoyed but definitely confused about her. He couldn't understand many of the things she did and said, nor what he did and said when he was around her. No wonder Sancia was so irritated when he showed up—he and Bibi acted like blubbering idiots together.

He slowly rose and began walking back but stopped at Achaz's cottage, which was in the same state as Marceline's. He pressed one hand against the door frame and began to sob. He wasn't sure why and yet deep inside he did. He felt he was constantly failing this man who had given all he had for Ferrelous to live. Ferrelous constantly wondered if he had been worth it. Often, as in this moment, he felt he was not.

He felt a hand on his shoulder and turned to see the sweet face of his mother looking up at him.

"I see you did a little too much thinkin'," she smiled, foggy-eyed.

He laughed and gave her a kiss on the cheek as he hugged this wonderful woman. How had he even considered Bibi to fill the shoes of this woman? He knew he wanted what his parents had—real love, the thoughtful kind.

"Come on. Let's go home. Father said he'd be home early tonight."

He grinned down at her mischievously.

"You're still the same hoodlum you always were. And always will be."

He laughed.

They walked happily home with their arms around each other. A pair of eyes gazed at them intently. They had been fixed on the boy sometime before Alura came. They belonged to a man who stood hidden from the passersby. He hoped to be able to talk with the lad tonight. He'd been on the verge of doing so when Alura, who he knew to be the lad's mother, had come.

He smirked, realizing this was no mistake. He was aware she knew he was getting impatient for Ferrelous to come into his own. He couldn't blame her for holding on to these last few days with her son. He did not envy her in the task that lay before her and her husband. Ferrelous was growing into a strong man—he would need to be. The man walked out into the light—it was Master Abrax.

He sighed as he gazed at this quaint place his brother had loved so dearly. He could see the same growing love in Sancia's eyes. It made little sense to him but, of course, that mattered little. He walked past the cottage the mother and son had entered without a sideward glance, and continued walking these streets he knew long ago had been walked by Achaz.

It touched his heart to see the lad weep at Achaz's door. He could only guess as to some of the reasons behind those tears. Ferrelous had never seen Abrax before, but he soon would be seeing a great deal of him. This reminded Ab of the many changes that lay ahead.

Life is often so tumultuous. It was good to be here in this quiet village with the soft rolling waves in the background. Perhaps this place made a little more sense to him than he thought.

He changed his course and soon entered his brother's cottage. In Achaz's Room of Knowledge he sat quietly, collecting his wandering thoughts. He walked over and saw the recently finished painting of him and

Sancia. He smiled, knowing she would be furious if she discovered he'd ruined the surprise. He would have to work on his pleasantly surprised face.

His eyes fell upon the new painting of her, and her parents and his smile acquired a deep sadness. She was such an amazing girl—a day hadn't gone by in which he wasn't reminded of it. He realized he should have discussed more with her of what she had read today. He should have talked to her about his father's death and explained to her more about the Volos. But he hadn't.

It was amazing how something that, at times, felt like another lifetime, could also feel as only moments away. He wondered if he would always feel this way—all indications pointed to 'yes', but indications aren't always foretelling, let alone prophetic. He looked around the room quietly, longing for things that could never be.

Then, he pulled the cloak he wore closer to him. Sancia lent it to him when he had a need for it, which he was thankful for. It would be hard to go back to any other form of travelling.

"Asulon Mansion, Bedroom," he said distinctly. He had never obtained the kind of intimacy with the cloak that Sancia enjoyed. He guessed this had something to do with being Mer or a descendent of

Baldoin. Probably both.

Sancia was still in the library with Gergo. He was sure they were still laughing over the good time they had earlier. Ab paced his floor as the future filled his mind. He was prepared for it, yet his intellect filled with various possibilities that would be out of his control. He abruptly stopped and let out a long breath. What was coming would come and there was no point in missing the present. He had done all he could; the rest he would have to trust the Creator.

He left his room and walked towards the library, carrying the cloak over one arm. There was no reason to become lazy just because he possessed such a teleporting marvel. As he neared the library, he could hear Sancia's laughter fill the hallway. This brought a grin to Abrax's face as he hoped there would never come a time when he didn't hear that laughter bouncing off these walls.

CHAPTER THIRTEEN

SORT OF

Sancia lay upon the grass in her front yard, gazing at the clouds roll by. She sighed a happy, lazy sigh, content with this moment.

"Well, what have we here?" a deep voice said, disturbing the silence. She smiled, knowing the voice all too well. She looked up to find the almos Gergo created when she was just a baby.

"Good morning, Elek," she laughed sitting up.

He came and lay beside her, and she began to stroke his mane. The bond between these two was resilient. Sancia felt she had a brother in him, which always made her smile, as she thought she was the only girl in the world with such a brother.

"So, are we just going to lie around all morning before you go off on your adventures in the Sea?" he asked, slightly jealous.

She knew it was rough for him because he wasn't allowed to go outside Asulon's grounds. He could fly as high as he liked, as long as he didn't cross the barrier into the outside world. Gergo and Abrax wished to keep the world in the dark as to Elek's existence for the time being.

"Let's fly!" she shouted, jumping onto his back. "Why watch the clouds when we can touch them!" he bounded off with a magnificent roar.

They rose higher and higher until the mansion looked like a little toy. Elek flew as swift as Sancia liked it, not as swift as he liked, which was much faster. Sancia held her arms out as if she herself possessed wings to fly. She couldn't imagine anything more wonderful than this moment. A playful smirk came across her face as she leapt from Elek's back and began to fall back towards the earth. She hardly made it a few seconds before he flew under her, and she was again on his back.

"Oh, come on, Elek!" she shouted, wishing he would let her fall for a little longer, but he never did.

"You know the answer," he returned with an amused look in his eyes.

"Fine," she murmured, then saw they were coming to a low cloud.

"Right there, right there!" she pointed excitedly.

"Alright. Hold tight and I'll spin through it."

An exuberant grin came across her face—she loved spinning almost more than she loved falling. They hit the cool wet air in the clouds and the world spun around them. Sancia shouted in glee. Elek laughed his deep chortle.

"We'd better get back," he said, knowing the reaction this would get.

"What? We just started!" she exclaimed.

"You know Master Ab doesn't like us flying too long," he answered obediently.

"Ugh! Fine; but someday we'll fly around the whole world," she said with determination.

She was increasingly growing more restless about only being allowed to go to Zacroon to spend time in the Sea or in the Room of Knowledge. The only people on land she was allowed to talk to was Alura and her husband, when he was rarely there . . .

Ferrelous too, but he didn't really count. She'd never even been into Redivivus. She didn't understand how Elek was able to stand being cooped up here like a caged bird. He never complained about it, though, not even to her. He was the more patient of the two.

As they returned to the ground, they saw Abrax watching them on his veranda with a smile on his face. He beckoned them to come to him. Elek landed softly beside him. Sancia slid from his back, still catching her breath from the amazing spinning.

"Did you enjoy yourselves?" Ab smiled seeing Sancia's flushed cheeks.

"Yes, Elek is getting better and better at flying all the time. You should see him when he doesn't have a rider. It's amazing!" she answered, leaning against Elek's soft fur.

"I believe he has a lot more in him than he shows," Ab replied as he looked at Elek pleased.

"I suppose we all have a lot more in us than we show," Elek answered thinking of his own Master Bence, who he hadn't seen since his early days and missed greatly.

"A true statement, my friend," Ab answered to the almos's humility; then turned to Sancia and asked, "Are you going to eat noonmeal here or with Bibi?"

"Oh, here, for sure," Sancia answered nodding her head assertively, "I cannot bear to eat another one of Bibi's attempts at seaweed muffins." She visibly sickened at the thought.

This made both Ab and Elek laugh, having heard already of Bibi's newfound passion for all things culinary, much to Sancia's dismay.

After mealtime was over, Sancia went to the Rose Room, which was now her room. The entire Flower Wing was her domain. She grabbed her cloak and tied the string loosely around her throat. She sat for a moment thinking.

This was the time she would go and spend a few hours in the Sea and then the rest of her time in her parents' cottage —her cottage now. The same old routine, just as she had done yesterday. Not to mention the day before and what seemed a thousand days before that. She then thought of today's flying with Elek being cut short and the feeling of being held back returned.

She sat a moment as her mind virtually trembled. She had never disobeyed her uncle before, but she was not a child anymore. He needed to see that she could handle herself as the young woman she now was.

"Redivivus," she whispered ever so softly.

She reappeared in between two buildings and was hidden from the view of the townspeople. She took a deep breath as she pulled her hood on and stepped out into the sunshine. The town's people were all a bustle, as was usual for them. A smile spread across her face as she saw them all at their various tasks, all of which appeared to be awfully important. She beamed as she slowly walked the street, watching them dash around.

Her eye caught on a young man leaning against a railing who was perhaps a year or two older than she was. He did not look like the Mer boys her age, who were all thin and lanky. He was rather too muscular for his age. His features were broad and jagged, and he had quite disarming light brown eyes framed with raven curly hair.

The reason her eyes caught on him was because his eyes were caught on her. She quickly glanced away and kept walking, wondering what this boy was doing, standing around while everyone else clearly had a million things to do. Even she was walking and gawking, not just gawking. Her heart began to race as she realized he had started to walk towards her, making her realize she very much preferred him simply gawking and not walking. She quickened her pace and hurriedly dodged into an alley.

"Sea," she whispered frantically.

The boy long gone, Sancia breathed heavily, wondering what in the world he had been about in following her. She thought of this for a moment and smiled as a thought entered her mind. Maybe he *liked her*. She burst out laughing, thinking of him entering the alley and finding that she was not there. She pictured his confusion, which made her laugh harder.

"What's so funny?" Bibi asked swimming up.

"Nothing. I just. . . Nothing," Sancia answered, regaining control of herself.

"Well, I'll tell you what's not funny. Ferrelous is *avoiding me*," Bibi said dramatically, brushing her mane of strawberry blonde hair back. She had grown willowy in figure and prized her long legs deeply.

"What do you mean?" Sancia asked irritated at the sound of Ferrelous's name from Bibi's lips.

"He has been in with Grandpa Audric all morning asking him all these questions about this and that. Does he think that I will just wait around forever? There are plenty of Mer boys who would love to be in his shoes and if he doesn't watch himself, they will be."

"All of them?" Sancia asked smiling.

"Maybe!" Bibi smirked impishly.

"You're pathetic, you know that?" Sancia chuckled.

"A little," Bibi laughed back. "Come on. I made some seaweed rolls that are supposed to be really healthy for you."

Sancia's stomach gurgled in protest, pleading its cause.

"Well, actually, I need to go and say hi to grandpa first," Sancia said quickly, "maybe I could send Ferrelous your way," she smiled, knowing this would seal the deal.

"Well, what are you waiting for? Swim!" Bibi answered as she whizzed off to freshen up.

Sancia smiled at her silly cousin who she couldn't help but love dearly. She entered the Castle and heard her grandfather's voice in the Throne Room. She entered and saw him with Ferrelous in deep conversation.

"Hello!" Sancia called out bringing both heads to attention.

"Aw, Sancia. How are you?" Audric said, immediately leaving Ferrelous and coming to his beloved granddaughter. Sancia smiled at Ferrelous's apparent irritation. He may be a great friend of her grandfather, but he was not even a close second to Sancia.

"Hello, Ferrelous," she smiled innocently.

"Hello," he answered dryly.

"Bibi's waiting for you at her house. I told her I would send you her way."

Ferrelous stood motionless as though he hadn't heard, "Right," he finally said, "I guess I'll be going then."

"Good chatting with you, Ferrelous. We can continue our conversation later," Audric smiled.

Ferrelous left with a gloomy look on his face. He couldn't believe he'd been outsmarted by a fourteen-year-old. Sancia wasn't a regular fourteen-year-old though; this thought helped ease the blow some.

He took a deep breath as he walked up to Bibi's house. Her pet fish whirled around him excitedly. He saw Bibi look out her window. He waved awkwardly. She didn't seem to notice and smiled brilliantly. Apparently, this was going to be harder than he thought.

"So you've come at last. I thought grandpa would never let you leave!" she said as she swam quickly towards him.

"Yeah. . ." Ferrelous muttered, not knowing how to do what he had to do.

"Well, I just made some seaweed rolls that are supposed to make your skin soft. Come in and try some," she said, taking his arm.

This information gave Ferrelous the courage he formerly lacked. Now that his heart was less involved his stomach had once again gained some ground.

"Actually Bibi, I came to talk to you," he said, coming to a stop.

"About what?" she asked curiously.

"About us . . . not being us . . . anymore," he answered slowly.

"What?" she laughed, slightly confused.

"I don't think we should, you know, be like *this* anymore. We should just be friends like we were before," he answered hopefully.

"What!" she shouted, no longer confused.

He sat there, not knowing what else he could say to make the matter more clear to her.

"Are you saying you don't *like me* anymore?" Bibi nearly screamed.

"Sort of," he answered as his voice became higher on the latter word.

"Sort of?" she fumed. "SORT OF!"

"I still like you as a friend," he said empathetically.

"Oh, do you?" she said, poking his chest threateningly, which at any other time he would have found humorous, but was currently terrifying. "Well, let me tell you something, *Ferrelous.* I never want to see your disgusting corpse here again. You come into this Sea, you stay as far away from me as possible or else!"

She finished, shooting him a pair of dagger eyes he was glad couldn't actually shoot daggers or he'd be a dead man.

She flew back inside the house sobbing without a backward glance.

"Well, that went. . . well," he mumbled.

"*Sort of,*" he heard from behind him and turned to see Sancia laughing at him with her eyes. *How do these girls do so many things with their eyes?* He marveled.

"Shut up! You don't know how hard that was," he said pointing his thumb back over the shoulder.

"I think I got a pretty good idea. Don't worry. She always reacts to things dramatically but she's usually fine afterwards. And word on the street is there are plenty of Mer boys lined up to fill your shoes," she remarked, smiling at her own inside joke.

"Well, I have to go," he said, looking nervously back at the house, taking no notice of what she had said.

"Shouldn't you wait so you can swim away as the sun sets? It won't be a true tragedy any other way," she said with a straight face.

"You think you're so funny, but we'll see who's laughing in a year or two, when it's your turn."

"It will still be me. You're not as funny as I am," she smiled sweetly as she patted him on the back and swam towards Bibi's front door.

"You're such a pest," he smiled in spite of himself. Sancia was many things, and clever was one of them.

"You still like me as a friend, though, right?" she laughed. "I've got some damage control to do so, if you'll excuse me. . ." She didn't wait for his reply as she entered the house of doom.

He swam off in a lighter mood than the one he'd been in before Sancia appeared. He hoped her first leap at love included a better landing than his. Somehow, he felt it would. He thought of Bibi poking his chest and this time the humor came to him. He chuckled his relief to have all that over with. As his thoughts then turned to the look in her eyes and her hysterical departure, his chuckle was abruptly halted.

He hadn't meant to hurt her. This experience made him realize he knew nothing about love and even less about the opposite sex. Maybe that's why he thought Sancia would have a better first go; she seemed to know more about both.

His thoughts turned back to what he and Audric had been discussing before Sancia interrupted them. Audric was just about to tell Ferrelous of the day he'd lost his wife. She literally had just disappeared one day, leaving no trace behind her.

Ferrelous had never broached the topic before because it was extremely painful for Audric. He wished more than ever Sancia had given them just a few more moments.

He felt for Audric and couldn't imagine what it must be like to always wonder, always hope for the best, always fear of the worst. What *happened* to her?

CHAPTER FOURTEEN

PROTECTOR OF SANCIA

Gergo stood gazing at the Mountains solemnly in the moonlight. Finn had reported the news that Andor had captured someone from Redivivus who was now being held captive in the Mountain. At least, that was the rumor going about the Mountains. Gergo's wrinkled brow furrowed as he sat in contemplation. They were becoming more daring in their midnight escapades. He clenched his jaw as he assessed the man he had become and the King he was ready to be. He knew the time had truly come.

His disguise swirled quickly around him and left Bence staring at his Mountain home with a foreboding look in his eyes. He heard a shout of alarm raise telling all those within and without the Mountains that *Bence* was back. He had prepared for anything except what happened next.

He saw three figures darting down the Mountain as though to hide not from him but from those around them on the Mountains. This was easy enough until they neared the foot of the mountain, where the trees grew more sparsely.

He watched intensely as the three sprinted frantically towards him. He wondered what they could be thinking. Surely, they didn't believe they could enter the yard and attack him? That would be utter stupidity on their part. He watched almost entertained until he saw others in pursuit of these three—not to go along, but to bring *them back.* At that moment, he knew they were not coming at him but to him.

He stood firm as he watched the pursuing group closing in on his new-found followers.

"Back," he said quietly but firmly, causing those in chase to come to an immediate halt. He watched them shudder in fear. This was not the disguised humiliated Bence they'd all been mocking only hours before.

This was Bence, King of the Artur, whom they had known in all his majesty. They dared not defy him without Andor. He watched as the three continued forward without so much haste, feeling the retreating of their former friends.

They came to the edge of the yard and stopped, not sure whether they could enter.

"You may enter," Bence heard from behind him. He turned to see Master Abrax smiling at this new course of events. Abrax knew Bence was prepared and ready to regain his rightful place as his rightful self —King of the Artur.

As the three walked hesitantly onto the yard, Bence recognized each one of them, one of which surprised him greatly—Ilona. He rushed forward to embrace each of them. The other two were Antal, his youngest brother, and a maiden whose name he could not recall in this overjoyed moment.

"You came!" he whispered fervently, first hugging Antal.

"Thanks to Katalin," Antal replied acknowledging the unnamed maiden.

"My thanks you will never know," Bence answered, taking the lovely lady's hand. She smiled happily without giving a reply. "Please tell me how this happened," Bence implored.

"Well, Andor was after her to be his bride, but she spurned him pretty soundly," Antal answered for her.

"So, he put her down in the cellar where all those turned to stone are being kept. He made some pretext about her being the only one who could break the Kovet Urlap. He would've had a riot on his hands for locking her away without some *gracious explanation*. The funny thing is he was right. She did break it, but only Ilona listened."

Bence turned confused to Master Abrax who was reasonably pleased with the tale told and not at all surprised by the events.

"She talked to us," Ilona explained. "It was strange being in that stone state. It's almost like not being alive at all. You aren't really a part of your surroundings and yet you are keenly aware of them. I heard Katalin talking about how Andor was no king. How we all were fooled into thinking we could usurp Bence's power. She talked and talked and talked till I couldn't stand it," Ilona laughed, causing Katalin to smile gently.

"At first, I was so angry at this girl who was plainly loyal to Bence. I wished I could do a great many harmful things to her. Then, she placed her hand on me, and I felt her warmth. It made me realize how cold I was, how terribly cold and hard I was compared to her hand. I no longer wanted to hurt her, I wanted to be like her. Soon, I was listening to what she was saying,

189

instead of merely hearing. She changed me back into myself, back into an Artur, a *real* Artur," she finished as tears fell from her grey eyes and she took her liberator's saving hand.

"I made a habit of coming down to visit Katalin, feeling pretty guilty for allowing her to be imprisoned in such a state. You can imagine my surprise today, when I found Ilona there with her," Antal laughed good-naturedly and went on, "I knew we couldn't stay there. Andor would use it to his advantage when he found that he was actually right about her. He truly believed those turned to stone were dead. I knew that, once he discovered the *means* of breaking Master Abrax's infliction, Katalin would be his prisoner for life. . . But you must know, Bence, that isn't the only reason I came. I have, for a long time, been no friend to Andor. But I played my part well enough, biding my time until an opportunity arose."

"And tonight, it did," Bence finished, wondering what falling out had occurred between Andor and Antal. Andor would rue the day he lost Antal as an ally.

Andor was cunning, but he was not keen; Antal was. Bence would discuss these things with his brother later.

"Bence," Antal said quietly as he knelt before his brother and King. "Can you forgive me for being a fool?"

"And I," Ilona echoed.

"And . . ." Katalin began.

"No, not you, Katalin. You were always loyal," Antal cut in before she could finish.

"Loyalty is an action as much as a feeling," Katalin replied humbly, taking her place beside her kneeling companions.

"I give you all my forgiveness and I ask yours in return, for being a weak King who led my people down a doomed path," Bence answered, as he also came down to his knees. Antal embraced the brother he dearly missed, Ilona hugged the friend she believed lost, and Katalin held the man she had never wavered from.

"I suppose you all will be needing a place to stay?" Abrax asked, cutting the moment short. "Can't be helped," he sighed, feeling the home he built for seclusion from the world seemed to be filling up with it.

"It would be too much to expect of. . ." Bence began.

"Oh, nonsense. It's the best way as long as Sancia is alright with it," Ab answered. "You three will wait here while Bence and I ask her. This is her house as much as mine, so the decision will be hers," he said, turning to go, but then turned back and said, "Should she allow it, I would say to all of you, especially to you,

Antal, if you so much as breathe wrong towards her, I will not simply change your connection with this world —*I will end it*." His blue eyes pierced them to their cores as he looked upon each, but especially to the one he named. "Do I make myself clear?"

They all nodded in terror of this being who they knew did not make empty threats. He entered the house with Bence following quickly behind. The latter realized Sancia would not recognize him or know him with his true appearance. This created something for him to fret about. As if he wasn't fretting enough after the severe warning his brother had just received. His mind returned to his surprise at seeing Ilona. He'd always believed that, once turned to stone, they were cut off from this world.

"Why didn't you tell me how the Kovet Urlap connection could be reversed?" Bence asked as they walked.

"You never asked," Abrax answered quietly.

"And?" Bence urged, knowing there was always more than one reason behind this man's actions.

"It wasn't only a test of their loyalty to you, but of your loyalty to them, as their King," he answered, maintaining his stoic walk.

Bence strode in silence as he pondered these words before he remarked upon them.

"It isn't an easy thing to be a King, especially when those you lead won't follow," Abrax said, observing Bence's mind at work. "I needed to know you were willing to be a King and not just a brother."

"I understand," Bence said somberly. "A King is held at a higher standard and expects a higher standard of those he leads than a brother and yet loves those he leads as a brother."

"Exactly," Abrax smiled. "I have never questioned your love for your people, but *true* love knows how to discipline and follow with greater love."

"Thank you for believing in me, not only as a man, but as a King," Bence said gratefully, knowing the love of which Abrax spoke was the love which he had given.

They entered the Flower Wing and walked quietly to Sancia's door. Bence hoped Sancia would take to his real appearance well.

"Sancia, may we come in?" Ab asked as he tapped on her door lightly.

"Sure," she answered sleepily.

The rose chandelier lit as Ab entered the room. Bence came in shyly behind him. Sancia's eyes grew wide when she saw this large handsome man enter her room. She pulled her covers to her chin. She thought it would only be Uncle Ab and Gergo.

193

"This is Bence," Uncle Ab said, "You know . . . the real Gergo?"

Sancia stared at Bence in open shock. Of course she had known Gergo's story and how he was in disguise. She hadn't realized how *much* of a disguise that was. She was suddenly so embarrassed of all the silly things she had done around him, like scaring him in the library; she was mortified. She took her eyes away from him as her embarrassment rose. She hadn't realized the real Gergo would be so attractive.

"Um, it's nice to meet you . . . I guess," she said awkwardly.

"Hey now, don't be like that," Bence said. "I'm still the same person; I just look different."

"Yeah! *A lot* different!" Sancia blurted.

"It's understandable if you think he's cute," Ab said seriously.

"Oh my. . . are you serious right now?" Sancia said, covering her face with her blankets. "That was *the* worst possible thing you could have said."

Bence started in surprise at Ab's remark. He shifted awkwardly, not knowing how he could ease the situation. He hadn't thought of her taking to his appearance too well.

"Listen, you may have *feelings* for me you didn't have before, but I want you to know I have always and will always see you as a daughter," he said reassuringly.

"Okay. *That* was the worst possible thing you could have said," Sancia moaned under her covers. Each man looked to the other for assistance, both being completely out of their element.

"Maybe I can help," they heard from behind them. They all turned and looked to see Katalin standing at the door. "I'm sorry to intrude but I had a feeling this might not go over well. Ilona told me to stay put but . . ." she didn't finish as her eyes fell upon Sancia. She saw the budding beauty without, but it was the beauty within she liked most.

"Oh, and I suppose you're the *real* Elek," Sancia said exasperated at another new face.

"No. My name is Katalin. I'm an Artur, like Bence. I just arrived with two others. But that really isn't important right now; what is important is what you're going through at this moment," Katalin said matter-of-factly as she came in closer. "Now, I'm going to ask you to indulge me for the next few moments. Do you think you can do that?"

"Sure," Sancia said eyeing this Katalin.

"I want you to look at Bence and think of Gergo. Now, Gergo looked like an old man, right?"

"Right."

"Well, Bence is an even *older* man. I want you to tell me the oldest person you know."

"My Grandpa Audric," Sancia said instantly.

Katalin smiled at his information. "Bence is almost the same age as your *Grandpa* Audric."

"Are you kidding?" Sancia asked, turning to Bence to rebuff this claim.

"It's true," he confirmed.

The look that came across Sancia's face told them that Katalin had hit her intended mark. Sancia sat in disgust not believing she had been attracted to someone practically as old as her *grandpa.* The thought itself sent a repulsive shiver up her spine. Abrax looked at Katalin with a newfound respect, and Bence with open awe.

"Oh, before I go, my friends and I were wondering if we could stay here for a while?" Katalin asked Sancia.

Sancia, in turn, left her bed, walked over to the tall woman, held out her hand and said, "You have no idea how long I've needed another woman around the house."

This caused all in the room to burst forth in laughter as the two shook hands happily. Abrax was still uneasy about the other two newly arrived guests in his home, but in Katalin he knew he had found another protector of Sancia. This was most welcome.

CHAPTER FIFTEEN

BRIGHT EYES

Sancia appeared animated in an abandoned Redivivus alley. Uncle Abrax had sent her off early, desiring her to be absent while he settled in the new arrivals. She hadn't even seen them except for, of course, Katalin, who, she believed, couldn't be topped anyways. Uncle Ab was not aware of the many visits she had made to this town or, greater still, that she'd been visiting here at all.

Her path had crossed with the brown-eyed boy's a few times since her first encounter. However, she'd skillfully been able to escape an interchange. It had become a sort of game she quite enjoyed.

She stepped out into the streets and was

surprised to discover an assortment of booths set up in the center of town. She never spoke to anyone but would nod and smile when appropriate. She eyed one booth covered with many flamboyant hats on display. She watched as the townsfolk bantered with the booth owners. It was entertaining to watch them go back and forth, and back and forth.

She neared the hat booth, observing the owner occupied in a lively exchange with a frumpy woman. It was apparent it would not be ending anytime soon. She picked up a small purple hat with large feathers attached to it. She wasn't sure if she liked it much. She'd never worn a hat before, so she wasn't certain how to judge their quality.

"Not your style," she heard directly behind her. Startled, she turned to find the brown-eyed boy smiling triumphantly at her. She may have won their many battles, but he had won the war. She wasn't sure if she was more happy or upset by this defeat.

"Are you an expert on these?" she asked, raising it.

"Naw, I don't pay much attention to hats."

"Well then, how would you know if it's my style or not?" she asked.

"Because I've paid attention to you and that hat isn't for you," he smiled as he took the hat from her hand and returned it to the booth.

"You're pretty smug, aren't you? Sancia asked, not impressed with his suave attitude. It told her this was not his first hat booth, let alone hat.

"No, I wouldn't say that. . . I'd say I trust my *intuition*. That's why I never have quit trying to talk to you," he smiled happily. She had to admit he did have a nice smile.

"Well, congratulations. Now you've talked to me. Have a hat," she said, handing him a hideous pink and orange one, then quickly walking away.

"Hey where are you going?" he asked, rushing up alongside her, hatless.

"I have other things to do today than talk about silly hats with silly people," she answered, giving him a sideward glance.

"Oh, are you so far above he?" he asked. "Who's smug now?"

"No!" she tried to rebound, realizing her hypocrisy. "I didn't mean it that way."

"Really? How did you mean it then?" he asked, folding his arms waiting for her explanation.

"I just meant that . . . well . . . I don't think I'm above you. I just have other things to do today."

"I don't know. I still think you meant that you are better than me," he answered unconvinced.

"Well, I don't think that," she answered, becoming agitated with him and with herself. Her behavior reminded her of *Bibi,* which was more than a little disheartening.

"Prove it."

"What?" she asked taken aback.

"*Prove it,*" he repeated distinctly.

"How?" she asked as a feeling of being ensnared crept up her spine.

"Simple. Take a walk with me to the river," he said.

"How would that prove I didn't think I was better than you?" she asked skeptically.

"You would prove *I* wasn't the silly person you were referring to when you said you had better things to do than talk to a silly person," he said beaming, recognizing his second victory.

She stared at him rather annoyed and tried to think of a rebuttal but couldn't seem to find one. This was somewhat due to the fact that part of her did not want to find one.

"Alright, but then, I really have to go," she said, conceding.

"Fine by me," he smiled, offering her his arm. She rolled her eyes but still took it amicably. A strange thing was happening to her —part of her was fighting and part of her was embracing. She wasn't sure which side was in the right.

They walked through the trees silently for a while; he wore a broad grin while his companion bore a furrowed brow.

"What are you thinking about?" he asked, detecting her mind at work. "I was thinking about my cousin if you must know," she answered as she realized this was the first person she'd ever talked to who wasn't family, or someone known by them.

"What about this cousin?" he asked.

"Just how she behaves in a certain aspect of her life and how I don't want to be the same way in that aspect of my life."

He looked at her confused but shrugged it off as they made their way deeper into the woods.

"What are you thinking about?" she asked, wondering if there was some code of conversation among strangers she was ignorant to, which included asking such questions.

"You don't want to know," he prodded teasingly.

"Oh," she replied, afraid she'd failed the code of conversation.

"I'm kidding," he said, nudging his elbow into her side.

"Oh," she repeated. *Real captivating, Sancia,* she thought.

"I was thinking about how glad I am you don't think you're better than me," he said, deciding to answer her question.

"That reminds me, why do you care whether I think I'm better than you or not?" she asked, as it occurred to her that this had confused her from the start.

"Well, I like you. I can tell your good opinion is one worth gaining," he answered, watching her reaction.

Her mind seemed to have stopped working. Previously, she had laughed at the idea of him liking her; now, she didn't understand what was so incredibly funny about it.

"Oh," she said again, to which he burst out laughing. "You're really funny. Before, you were all about telling me what was what, and now, I can't get more than one word out of you."

"Well, you said your *intuition* wanted to talk to me, not me to talk to you," she smirked up at him, finally regaining her wits.

"Alright, alright. I surrender," he said holding his hands up.

"It's about time but, I have to admit, you were a worthy opponent," she laughed, relaxing a little. "How far is the river?" she asked, realizing they had come a good distance from the town.

"Just up around the bend," he said. "What, are you getting tired of my company?"

"No. I just have never been to the river before," she answered. They walked around the bend and she saw the rushing water ahead of her. She smelled its fresh scent in the air and gazed as it whipped over the rocks. She released the boy's arm and walked closer to the water.

"It's beautiful," she said, watching the foaming water swirl.

"I thought you'd like it. That's why I suggested we come here."

"Why did you think I'd like it?" she asked, turning to him inquisitively.

"Intuition again, I guess," he smiled as he walked toward her and the water.

She didn't believe his answer. She felt as though there was something more to all this than his supposed savvy intuition. She thought of Elek's words about how everyone has parts of them they don't show. Sancia knew that, in time, these parts are revealed one way or another.

"I just realized I don't even know your name," she said.

"Bolek," he answered. "Yours?"

She hesitated, not knowing if she should say, in case it got back to her uncle. "I think I better get going. . ." she said without answering and turned to leave.

"Come on, I told you my name," he said, standing in front of her. She tried to walk around him, but he grabbed her playfully.

"Um . . . How about for now you just give me a nickname," she continued, as she tried to pull away from him.

"You really won't tell me your name?" he asked. She shook her head she would not and then looked up at him to see what he would do. "Alright. Well, then. . . I guess I'll call you. . . Cloaky Croaky." He tried to hold a straight face.

Sancia burst out laughing, "That's the best you've got?" She had not been expecting something quite that ridiculous.

"I thought it to be very fitting," he said in pretend defense. "Fine. If you really don't like it, I guess I can come up with another one. . ."

Still laughing, she looked up at him expectantly. He sat there, staring into her eyes without saying anything, until Sancia grew uncomfortable and dropped her gaze.

"Bright Eyes," he said smiling again.

"Tacky," she smirked, as she tried to pull away from him again.

"It's your fault for looking so tenderly at me," he teased awaiting her response, which came immediately.

"What? If anyone was looking tenderly, it was you!" she answered defensively.

"I'm glad you noticed," he said, as he tightened his grip.

"Let go of me, Bolek," Sancia said, looking at him with far from a tender look.

"Why, what's wrong?" he smiled his charming grin.

"You didn't bring me out here because you thought I'd like it. You brought me out here because you knew we'd be alone and thought I'd swoon at your charms. Well, you thought wrong," she said, pushing herself away with much more strength than before.

"No, I didn't," he said, releasing her immediately. "I really just wanted to get to know the girl in the cloak who always somehow disappeared into thin air. I'm sorry if I got a little . . . .excited . . . I'm sorry." She looked at him and didn't know if she believed him or not. She needed to go someplace where she could collect her thoughts, to think this whole situation out fully, without him staring at her.

"I really need to go," she said, quickly walking away from him.

"Can I see you again?" he asked timidly. "I really am sorry."

"Maybe," she answered and then ran off before he could say another word. Once she was out of his view, she whispered cottage, and soon she was safe in the Room of Knowledge, where she hoped she could again see clearly.

He didn't run after her this time, knowing it would only drive her away more. Why was it this girl seemed to be always outside his grasp? She was one smart cookie, inexperienced, yes, but very smart. He hoped he hadn't botched things up so badly that she would never come to Redivivus again.

That could make things very difficult for his current goals. He knew he must be patient. He thought of her answer—Was that a maybe to seeing him again, or a maybe to him being sorry? *Very smart indeed*, he smiled.

CHAPTER SIXTEEN

A SOLON'S FURY

Antal sat listening to Bence as he related the life he had led since leaving their home. He recognized how much Bence was changed from the man he had been when Antal had last seen him. There was a new depth to Bence which Antal couldn't grasp completely. Antal found Bence to be a better man than he'd ever been. The role of a servant had taught Bence that a King is a servant to all those he leads.

Bence introduced him to Elek, who received both Ilona and him markedly coolly. He could see the amazing creature was especially loyal to his brother. He'd allowed Katalin to touch his wings, which both he and Ilona longed to do. It would take a great deal for the almos to trust any of them.

Antal added him to the growing list of persons who didn't trust him. He inquired why Bence had not created a female, to which he learned Master Abrax wished him to wait.

The thought of Master Abrax reminded him of the stern warning he had received. Andor was a hard nose, but Antal never feared him. Master Abrax was another case entirely.

"Well, it's dinnertime," Bence said, beckoning his friends to follow him. They had been shown some of Asulon's Wings but not all. Antal felt as though he was walking on glass, which would at any moment shatter under his weight.

"Do you always dine with Master Abrax?" Katalin inquired.

"Yes, most of the time. I prepare his meals and keep the house in order. He likes company, even though he won't admit it," Bence smiled, thinking of the many proofs of this.

"Are you sure he wants *our* company, though?" Antal asked, speaking mostly of *his* company.

"He told me he would like everyone to be there. His reasons are his own," Bence replied.

They entered the Silver Dining Hall which was

Abrax's favorite Dining Hall in the house.

"Come in, come in," he said, having, as was tradition, already begun his meal.

"Thank you," Bence said cheerfully, even though it had not been him to whom Abrax was referring.

The others took their places and sat quietly while Bence and Abrax chatted away about subjects of which the others were mostly ignorant.

Sancia appeared beside Abrax, causing all of them, except Abrax, to start in surprise.

"Oh, I'm sorry. I forgot we had guests," Sancia said embarrassed.

"Sancia," Abrax said sternly. "What are you doing home so soon? You were supposed to be dining with Audric this evening." He was not pleased as he watched his guests' reactions intensely.

Ilona was much less affected than Antal, who was trying hard not to gawk.

"I . . . I need to talk to you," Sancia said, ringing her hands nervously. Abrax noted this behavior and immediately rose from his place. He placed a hand on her cloak, and she whispered, "Library." They were gone.

"That's a nice trick," Ilona smirked, then continued eating, finding food to be exceptionally delicious after being a stone for so long.

"It is," Bence answered, watching Antal closely. "How are you doing there, Antal?"

"I wish . . . she hadn't entered . . . that way," he gasped, trying to calm himself now he was not under Abrax's eye.

"I'm surprised by how affected you are," Bence frowned. "She's a *child*."

"When was the last time you looked at that girl?" Antal answered. "She may not yet have bloomed, but she's far from a seedling."

Ilona and Katalin chuckled to one another at this.

"It's no joke!" Antal responded angrily.

"Antal, the girl is clearly beautiful but honestly man, pull yourself together," Ilona smirked teasingly.

"Tell me truly, Antal," Bence questioned, taking on a very sober air, "Are you a threat to Sancia?"

"No. I wouldn't stay if I thought myself to be one," Antal answered truthfully. He had seen the damage he was capable of wreaking. This guilt was a saving grace from himself.

Bence looked closely at Antal, who he could now see bore many of his own self-inflicted wounds trying to heal. He nodded, believing the words his brother had spoken. A sensation swelled in him of the need to help his youngest brother as best as he could.

His thoughts then turned to Sancia and her

211

strange behavior. He wondered as to the subject of the conversation now taking place in the library.

Abrax had just finished scolding Sancia for her abrupt entrance. Considering he already had explained quite clearly that she would be meeting their new guests in a controlled manner, he was quite upset with her behavior.

"I'm sorry, but I was sitting in the cottage, and I realized I've done something really stupid; something you probably wouldn't have even cared about if I had just asked. And I feel horrible for not telling you and now I'm so confused, and I don't know what to do and I know you'll know what I should do. But it's going to be so *awkward* to talk to you about, especially after last night's episode," she rattled out. Abrax sat there perplexed as she chattered on rapidly, feeling his heart rate increase.

"What is this stupid thing you have done?" he asked calmly.

Sancia sat for a moment, wondering if she had done the right thing in choosing to tell him. It was too late to turn back now.

"I've been going to Redivivus before I go to the Sea and the cottage," she blurted out.

"I see," Abrax answered, feeling his anger rising.

"I know I shouldn't have done it, but I just feel

like I'm old enough now. I mean, you were two years younger than me when you left on your own. I feel like you're trying to box me into this place," she said waving her arm to show she meant Asulon. "I know you love me and you're trying to protect me, but you can't protect me from *everything.* You have to let me fall down if I'm every going to learn how to stand up."

"So, this is my fault?" he asked tersely.

"No. It's not your fault. I'm just trying to explain why I did what I did. But I actually didn't come here to tell you about that."

"Oh please, do continue," he said sarcastically. Sancia noticed the pained look he was fighting to conceal.

"I'm so sorry!" she cried, hugging him. "You have done so much for me and have always given me everything. I'm so selfish." She wept bitterly on his shirt and couldn't help but think of her parents and what a disappointment she was.

"Hey now," Abrax said, trying to soothe her. "It's alright. I forgive you. I suppose I've been perhaps a *little* overprotective, but that's because I know what I'm protecting you from."

"I know," she said smiling, grateful to have someone who loved her enough to take that responsibility on.

213

"Tell me about your trips to ol' Redivivus," he smiled sitting in his chair.

"Well, that's actually what I want to talk to you about," she said, feeling the same nervousness come back.

"I'm all ears," he said encouragingly.

"Well, I really like it there. The people are so funny. They hustle around, waving and shouting out to one another. It's a nice place and every time I've gone, it's been different and yet the same," she paused, musing over this.

"How long have you been going there?"

"A little less than two weeks. Sometimes, I've gone more than once a day. But I always had my hood on so people couldn't see my face unless they looked closely. I didn't want to be recognized."

"Cautious," he smiled, trying to picture her among the crowd in her hooded cloak in the blazing sun, completely inconspicuous.

"I was. That's why whenever Bolek tried to talk to me, I'd run into an alley and disappear," she added, feeling he understood how hard she really had tried.

"*Bolek?*" he asked abruptly, becoming much more serious.

"Yes. He's this boy who's been trying to talk to me because of *his intuition,*" she mimicked his deep voice

214

and then went on, "Today he did because I was looking at a hat booth. He said it wasn't my style, the hat I was holding, not the booth. Then I asked why. That's where the intuition part comes in. Anyways, he ended up tricking me into going on a walk with him to the river. So, we go to the river and he's trying to be really charming about everything. I wouldn't tell him my name, so he grabbed me," if Sancia had been paying attention, she would have seen her uncle's apparent flinch and certainly would have treaded more lightly as she went on. However, she did not, and probably for the best.

She continued, "So he made up some silly nickname, Bright Eyes, which was actually the second one. So that got him into saying I was looking *tenderly* at him, which I wasn't. Then, I think he was going to try and kiss me, but I stopped him and told him he was a . . . sleaze. He said he wasn't and then said sorry and asked if I would see him again. I said maybe and then went to the cottage and now I'm here. I haven't eaten since breakfast . . . I didn't even go to the Sea," she remarked troubled, now realizing her grandpa would be worried. She was slightly out of breath as she took notice of her uncle's expression for the first time.

"This *Bolek* is in Redivivus?" Ab asked, his blue eyes aflame.

"Yes . . . but he didn't hurt me," Sancia said

frightened.

"Give me your cloak," he said rising.

"W. . .hy?" she stuttered.

"Sancia, I need you to go to your room. Bence will bring you your meal," he steadily answered without answering her question.

"You're not going to hurt him, are you?" she asked.

"Go to your room," he said as he kissed her forehead, which soothed her until she again saw the look in his eyes. She had laid the cloak on the table, and he picked it up and draped it around himself. It adjusted itself accordingly to its wearer. She paused before leaving the room.

"It was my fault. I should've just talked to him in the first place instead of turning it into a game," she said.

"I'll be back soon," he smiled, knowing this was anything but her fault. When she left, he quickly appeared in the Dining Hall.

"Take Sancia her dinner and guard her door."

"I'm not going to hurt her," Antal said exasperated at having to go over this again.

"It's not you I'm worried about," Abrax said.

It was at this moment that they caught the faint glow Abrax's eyes were emitting. Bence immediately went into action. The others followed him quickly as he sent them to different posts for further protection. Each ever so thankful they were not the target of a Solon's fury, especially when that Solon was Master Abrax. His fury already had accomplished an impressive feat — clearing out a room of Artur.

Abrax listened as they hurriedly went into action. He stood for a moment, breathing deeply, knowing it would be important for him to be as calm as possible. He wished he could be more like his father, who had always been calm. *Always.*

He closed his eyes and pictured his father's face. He could hear his words, which he often spoke to him, *Be strong, son, Solon Strong*. When he opened his eyes, they shone about their rims and from their pupils, and finally eased back into their usual state.

"Redivivus," he said with a frightening calmness.

CHAPTER SEVENTEEN

THE CABINETMAKER'S SON

Alura sat gazing around her home, which had been filled with so many happy memories for so many years. Her mind rolled through Ferrelous's life and the man he had become. She was waiting for him and her husband to get back from their evening walk. She'd prepared one of Ferrelous's favorite meals for supper. A tear escaped her eye, which she wiped away quickly. She needed to keep it together, they would be home soon. The next day would be Ferrelous's eighteenth birthday.

They would spend the morning celebrating, the afternoon talking and the evening packing. By nightfall, he would be gone. She knew Master Abrax would be punctual and expect them to have their goodbyes out of the way. She smiled, thinking of the other night when he tried to talk to Ferrelous before the time was right. It very much irritated her at the time.

She knew these last hours must be filled with happiness for all of them to fall back on in the coming days. She heard the familiar sound of their laughter and smiled. They entered in this jovial manner, removing their boots and jackets by the door as Alura had long ago trained them to do. Her husband was holding up well, even though she knew this was equally as hard on him as on her.

"Had a good time then, I take it?" she smiled, placing the steamy food on the table.

"Yes. Dad was telling me about market today," Ferrelous laughed, still thinking over the stories and then glanced at the table full of food. "This looks great!"

"Well, sit up then so we can dig in," Alura's husband said, already sitting at his regular spot. He was a large man with a large smile he often shared.

"Hungry, Al?" Alura smiled.

"Starvin'," he patted his stomach, grinning at his wife. She was just a petite little thing who somehow was able to keep two brutes in line.

They all sat down to enjoy the hearty meal. The men thanked Alura for the hard work she had put into preparing the meal. The fire in the hearth warmed the air around them, causing the cottage to feel even cozier than it already was. Alura gazed between these two manly faces that were her life. She couldn't fathom what life would be without one of them—she didn't want to. Soon, it would be reality.

"I just remembered somethin' else that happened today!" Al cried, shocked he'd forgotten this tale to be told.

"What?" Ferrelous asked excitedly.

Al rubbed his hands eagerly together and then began, "Today, before I went into market, I went aboard Brun's ship because he just had a stunnin' new cabinet put in, which, I might add, he's been braggin' round town about since he first came up with the idea of puttin' it in. Anyways, he's settin' out to Sea today and wanted me to see it before he went. Now, do you remember Brun's twin sister, Bernia?" Al paused as he looked at Ferrelous.

"Is it possible to forget her?" Ferrelous snorted, thinking of the fiery young woman he'd learned long ago to steer clear of.

"Well, then you remember how she never fails in tryin' to stow away on Brun's ship before every voyage?"

"Why he doesn't just take her with him I'll never know," Alura rolled her eyes exasperatedly.

"Because she's plum crazy, that's why," Ferrelous answered.

"Anyways. . ." Al cut in, wanting to continue on with his story. "We walk into his cabin, and he walks me over to this massive cabinet, which is really much more like a closet if you ask me. As we come closer, we see what appears to be a lady's skirt stickin' out of the bottom."

"Bernia," Ferrelous hooted.

"Yes! The best part is the skirts had jammed the doors shut tight. Apparently, she'd been in the process of tryin' to find a place to hide in his cabin when she heard us comin'. So she fled to the cabinet and got her skirts stuck in the process. Brun and I tried for a good half hour without so much as budgin' it, him hollerin' at her the whole time and she hollerin' back. Oh. . ." he said wiping the tears of glee from his eyes, "I wish you would've seen Brun's face when he saw those skirts in his brand new cabinet. It took every ounce of self-control I had not to bust my gut right then and there. Oh, and she says to Brun when we can't open the door, *For the record, this was all part of my plan,*" Al said, mimicking Bernia's voice.

"Did they get her out?" Alura asked concerned.

"Yes, they did," Al smiled easing his wife's worries. "Brun had to have the cabinet maker come and

221

cut the door off because he'd had it specially made so when locked it couldn't be gotten into. How was he supposed to know there'd be ways to lock it without using a key?" He and Ferrelous laughed heartily while Alura chuckled, shaking her head.

"What happened when they got her out?" Ferrelous asked.

"Oh, she was ready for Brun. She did feel sorry for ruinin' his precious cabinet. She told him she was sorry for the cabinet, but it was his fault for never lettin' her go out to Sea when the ship was just as much hers as his."

"Which is true," Alura cut in, knowing it had been inherited by both of them from their grandfather.

"Yes. But it's Brun's crew who sails the ship," Al added. He went on to finish his tale, "To end happily, Brun promised to take her on his next voyage, which she made him sign a contract to do, clearly having heard such promises before. The cabinet maker said he could replace the door when Brun got back from his voyage. And last, but assuredly not least, Brun gets one last voyage without Bernia."

"Not quite happily ever after though, is it?" Ferrelous smiled.

"Perhaps it will be," Alura answered. "Bernia's

222

temper's mostly been about the ship. Maybe once she has that, she'll settle down. I think her, Brun, and the cabinet will come out just fine," Alura gleamed amused.

"To the cabinet of peace," Al raised his glass.

"The cabinet of peace!" Ferrelous and Alura cried, raising their own glasses. They all burst out laughing at their own joke.

Ferrelous looked at his parents and felt an amazing amount of gratitude fill his heart. He thought of Sancia, who'd lost her parents, one of which had been his fault. He wondered for the first time how he would treat the person who caused one of his parent's death.

A deeper level of respect for Sancia came over him as he realized she was a superior person to himself. He realized if such a thing ever happened, he didn't know if he could forgive that person, let alone be their friend. She really was the great granddaughter of Marceline and the daughter of Achaz and Jacqueline.

"Wasn't your dad a cabinet maker?" Ferrelous asked his dad as his thoughts returned to the story.

"Yes. He was and a plum good one too," Al answered proudly.

"Why didn't you become a cabinet maker?"

223

Ferrelous inquired, realizing he'd never thought of this before.

"Well, my father quit it around the time I was born. I was the last one of the brood and my dad had a lot on his hands when I was born. Oh, he would sometimes make small things for us kids, but my older brothers took over the business."

"Was he old when you were born?" Ferrelous asked confused.

"Old inside, I think," Al said taking on a much more serious tone. "He'd gone through and lost an awful lot by the time I come around. But he was still a great man and great dad to me."

"It's a shame he gave it up before you could learn the trade though," Ferrelous said, thinking it would have been nice to learn the art of wood.

"To be honest, I really had no desire to join in my brothers' lot. I respect the trade and see the beauty in it, but my hands were much better suited to weave nets than carve wood," Al mused. "Plus, I never would've caught this beauty and that would've been the greatest loss of all," he finished, taking Alura's hand.

"Is that why you left the village you grew up in? I mean, about the desire, not about mom," Ferrelous asked smiling.

224

Alura sat silently listening to this interchange, knowing its significance for what tomorrow would bring.

"It was one of the reasons. You see, my father died when I was around your age. My brothers were all married and livin' their own lives by that time. My mother left my father when I was still a toddler. I felt the call of the Sea and my brothers wished me well. I truly was guided to this place, which I now call home."

"Do all your brothers live in that village still?"

"All except one," Al answered, glancing quickly at Alura and felt her gently press his hand. Ferrelous waited expectantly for an explanation.

"My oldest brother left our village when I was still a boy."

"Where did he go?"

"I'm not sure, to be honest with you. I was very young, but I still remember his goodbye to me. I didn't realize he would never be comin' back. He seemed to believe he would someday. Perhaps he did make it back, only I wasn't there to meet him. . . He was my hero though," Al smiled sadly, trying not to dwell on this painful memory. "I thought the world of him, and he tried to spend a lot of time with me, even though I was ten years younger than him. I missed him sorely when he left; still do."

"How old was he when he left?"

"He left the night of his eighteenth birthday," Al said as he began to help Alura clear the table.

Ferrelous sat contemplating this history his father had just related to him. He couldn't help but feel a kind of contempt for this older brother who had left his family, more particularly his dad. He had never asked much about his father's family because he knew it was painful for his father to talk about. His dad liked to focus on happy memories and there didn't seem to be many found in his former life.

"It's funny, isn't it, that you were the one your father named after himself?" Ferrelous questioned thinking out loud. "I mean, you had all these brothers before you, but it was the last son he chose to bear his name."

"I think it's because I took after my father more than my brothers did," Al answered and then went on, "I'm glad of it, though, I've always thought Alder to be a strong name."

"Did grandpa like it too?"

"I think so or at least, I hope so. Wouldn't say much about me if he didn't like the name, would it?" Alder joked, causing both Alura and Ferrelous to join in his chuckle. He always was able to make even his darkest moments light. Alder's father had chosen wisely—Al was a credit to the Alder name.

Al thought of his given name and what he hadn't shared with Ferrelous concerning it. It was true he had been given it because he did take after his father a great deal more than his brothers. But a larger part of why it was given to him was because his mother had been against naming any of their sons Alder.

Not because she possessed a problem with the name, or with the Cabinet Maker she'd married who bore it. No. Her problem dealt with what came with the name. She swore if a child of hers bore this name she would leave. She'd been true to her word.

Al often wondered whatever became of her. He'd grown knowing his brothers blamed him for her loss and envied him as the bearer of their father's name, whereas they could only bear his business. This was why Al mourned the loss of his eldest brother so keenly. He'd been the only brother from whom Al never felt resentment.

Al watched his son's grin and thought of this brother. He remembered well the last night he'd spent with him was much like this one. He remembered also the goodbye and knew this goodbye would be all the more agonizing than the first. Seconds usually are harder than firsts when it comes to things such as this.

CHAPTER EIGHTEEN

BOLEK

Abrax appeared in Redivivus, where the streets were now mostly empty. The booths had long been packed up and locked down, with their owners bedded in for the night at a local inn or tavern. Abrax walked steadily past these in the direction of the river.

He occasionally would stop, close his eyes and then continue onward. He went on a small way into the woods when he saw off in the distance a small house, sadly neglected in its appearance. If it weren't the light coming from the small front window, one would have thought it long ago abandoned.

He was glad of its location being a nice distance from the main town. Seclusion was what he desired most for this meeting between him and *Bolek*.

Abrax walked up to this house and stood still for a moment, collecting himself. When he felt this accomplished, he tore the door from its place and flung it against a neighboring tree. He saw the frightened Bolek clumsily rise from the spot where he had been sleeping beside the fireplace.

"Good evening, Bolek. Did I wake you?" Abrax asked calmly.

"Are you out of your mind?" Bolek asked, trying to regain his composure.

"No. I wouldn't say so. I've experienced the state of being outside my mind and this is not it," Abrax answered.

"Listen, I don't know who you are but. . ."

"But I know who *you are*, Bolek—more importantly, I know *what* you are," Abrax cut in.

"I don't know what you're talking about," Bolek returned, becoming much more frightened than at the start of their conversation.

"Oh, but you do, don't you, *Bolek*. Honestly boy, if you're trying to hide, change your given name."

"I didn't think anyone here would recognize it. I

mean, why would the Terra here be familiar with anything about. . ."Bolek cut himself off.

"The *Volos*?" Abrax nearly spat, causing Bolek to flinch.

"Listen, I know I come from a pretty twisted lot, but that doesn't mean I myself am twisted," Bolek pleaded.

"You listen to me," Abrax demanded, grabbing the young man's collar, "You stay away from my niece. I know what you come from, and I know what you're capable of. But hear me when I tell you, you are nothing against me. Yours have been an enemy to my people for an awfully long time. Aw yes, I see the realization coming to you. Yes, I am Solon, but not a very *good* one. Do you understand?

"I've never heard of anything but a good Solon," Bolek answered, trying to match Abrax's eyes but failing.

"You are hiding something, Bolek, and not just your identity," Abrax remarked, ignoring this pathetic attempt at distraction. "I know it has something to do with my niece. You didn't just pick her out because of her cloak. That may have given her away, but it's not why you're here. Is it, Bolek? I have my theories as to what you're after, but I will find the truth. In that aspect, I am an exceptionally good Solon."

He released Bolek's collar and then went on, "Now, do you want to enlighten me, or do you want to drag this out?" Arbax asked almost too coolly.

Bolek stood for a moment, contemplating this man's words. He was very sick of being bullied around by people who thought they were better than him. He looked at this man who he knew was extremely powerful—he practically emitted the stuff. He let out a big sigh and then spoke.

"It's not that simple."

"Go on."

"Listen, I didn't come here on some kind of mission the Volos have for her. If they have one, I wouldn't know about it because I ran away when I was twelve. I came here and thought it was a great place until one night one of those Artur found me. Obviously, he recognized me for what I am and wanted to be an *ally* was the word he used. But really, I just have ended up having to do what he says. I didn't want to because I know the Artur and the Volos are practically fused at the hip these days, but he threatened to expose me if I didn't. I knew I wouldn't get far once that happened. So, I gave in," Bolek explained.

"His name?" Abrax asked.

"What?"

231

"The name of the Artur man who enlisted your services."

"He said his name was Bence."

"*What*?" Abrax asked as his chest tightened.

"Bence. The man who came here said his name was Bence. You know, like their King? But I don't think this guy is their King; just someone named after him."

"What did he look like?" Abrax asked, trying to control his voice.

"Really tall; he has blonde hair and is pretty lanky for an Artur. Has a face that would scare small children," Bolek clarified.

Abrax relaxed a great deal and was somewhat ashamed of himself for nearly believing the worst in his long-time friend. He was glad he hadn't overreacted.

"The man with whom you have had dealings is not Bence but Andor," Abrax corrected.

"You mean as in real Bence's brother?" Bolek asked shocked.

"Yes."

"You've got to be kidding me," Bolek huffed, sinking down onto an old wobbly wood stool.

"I wish I were," Abrax said. "What was this plot he had for my niece?"

232

"Well, he never really told me the whole thing. He just wanted me to talk to her, you know, get to know her. He said it was important for her to trust me. He made it sound like she needed to be protected," Bolek finished, looking up at Abrax, disappointed with himself.

"Well, I can assure you he was right about that," Abrax said, his anger rising once again. He wondered if Antal knew about this plot. If he did and hadn't told Abrax, it would not bode well. "How often do you see Andor?"

"He comes every night. That's one of the reasons why I tried so hard to talk to her. I mean, I wanted to talk to her for me too, but he would come and be so upset each time I told him that I hadn't talked to her. I was waiting for him before you came. . . Well, before I fell asleep," Bolek answered, wishing all these uninvited guests would leave him alone.

This information was upsetting to Abrax, who realized that, if Andor himself was coming here every night, Sancia was a top priority to him. He wondered who had informed Andor of Sancia's cloak. He must have spies working for him during the daytime. It was obvious that Andor assumed Sancia would eventually visit the town, so he had enlisted the naïve Bolek. How rightly the braggart had guessed.

Abrax walked to the door and gazed out through the woods. He spotted someone trying to hide behind a particularly wide tree a slight distance away. He would have been amused if he wasn't so irate, "I can see you, Andor."

The dark shape flitted off, dodging behind trees as it went, as though expecting some sort of attack. Bolek joined Abrax in the doorway and began laughing incredibly loud as he saw the lanky shadow retreat.

"How did you do that?" Bolek asked amazed, "For the life of me I couldn't get him to stay away."

"Really?" Abrax asked surprised. "Why didn't you shapeshift into some malicious beast? Most likely would've done the trick."

"I don't shapeshift. Haven't since I left Volos City," Bolek answered stiffly, losing his former joviality.

"Why not?" Abrax pressed.

"Because. . . I've seen the worst in every shape," Bolek replied, quietly leaving the door. "That's why I'm glad we can only replicate animals and not people like you and the Artur. Well, when the Artur were still the Artur."

"Why is that?" Abrax asked, desiring to understand the workings of this young Volos's mind.

234

"Do you know what a Volos would do with that ability? They would turn into someone's father, or sister, or lover, just to torment the person and then eventually kill them in that form," Bolek answered with a haunted look in his eyes, which affected Abrax greatly. Abrax had witnessed but one killing done by a Volos, from which he'd never fully recovered. He could not imagine the horrific things this boy had witnessed and lived through.

"I need you to tell me everything Andor told you about my niece," Abrax demanded, knowing he must keep his focus.

"Honestly, he didn't tell me very much. He just said to keep an eye out for a girl in a dark blue hooded cloak. She wouldn't talk to anyone but would probably be very interested in everyone," Bolek explained, "I'd been on the lookout for about two months with no luck and then, she just appeared one day. Well, once I saw what she *looked* like . . ." he stopped, seeing the threatening look Abrax gave him and went on more carefully. "I mean, once I saw her, I was more motivated to talk to her because I knew she was the girl I was supposed to get to know," he tried to smooth over, unsuccessfully.

"Anything else you think I ought to know?" Abrax asked, searching the boy's face for any hint of deceit.

"To be frank, I think you already know everything I think," Bolek said under the scrutinizing glare. "If anything comes to mind, I'll let you know. I should tell you though, I won't talk about Volos City."

"Why?" Abrax pushed.

"I guess I should say, I can't. . . talk about it. There's a reason I left when I was twelve. I'll just leave it at that," he said, clenching his jaw and swallowing hard.

Abrax was struck by the similarity he held with this boy. There also had been a reason he left at the age of twelve. A reason he still didn't talk about and for a long time couldn't talk about.

"What are you going to do now Andor is no longer your *ally*?" Abrax asked, afraid of what he was getting himself into.

"I suppose I'll have to try and move on somewhere else before the Volos come to *retrieve* me," Bolek chuckled mordantly.

"I know where you can go," Abrax sighed.

"Where?" Bolek asked surprised.

"Zacroon," Abrax said. "I have just the cottage for you, which will be lent to you on the condition you keep it in its current state and not this one's."

"That's by the Sea, isn't it?" Bolek asked curiously.

"Yes. This particular cottage belonged to my niece's grandmother. It has certain protections placed on it, so you shouldn't have to worry as long as you're in it. I'm quite certain you'll be safe there, as Zacroon is under King Audric's protection as well."

"Are you sure he'll be ok with protecting a Volos?"

"Trust me, of the two of us, I'm the one who has more reservations on that account."

"So, I guess it would be a bad idea to ask if I could see your niece again?"

"A very bad idea," Abrax answered without so much as an amused twinkle in his eye.

Bolek nodded awkwardly, his hopes dashed. For a moment, he thought this Solon was actually taking to him. Either way, he was thankful for all the man was doing for him. It was more than anyone had ever done in his entire life.

"Thank you for helping me. No one's ever done that for me before and it means a lot. Your niece is lucky to have you," Bolek said and paused before he went on, "I know what I am better than anyone, but I also know what I'm not. The Volos *were* good at the start of the world, maybe not very long after, but no one was created to be bad. They became bad. Anyways, I just want to tell you I'm thankful you didn't rough me up or kill me. I have no doubt you could've done both if you'd let

237

yourself."

"Part of me hopes one day you know how difficult it is for me to help you, and the other part hopes you never find out," Abrax answered.

Then, he touched the boy with part of the cloak and said, "Marceline's Cottage, Zacroon."

They reappeared in Marceline's bare cottage which had been left very much as it was after she died. It was clean, being recently dusted. Bolek looked around, appreciative of this place, which far exceeded his last residence.

"This is really nice. It's got a really good feeling about it. Like you know the people here were really happy before you know . . . they left," Bolek finished clumsily.

"It is a very special place to me and to this town. You must respect it and keep it just as it is. I'm not sure how the town will react to having someone actually living here, but I don't think they'll be unfriendly."

Bolek nodded, not quite understanding what was being said to him. "I'll take really good care of it," he said, looking the cottage over again. "Do you think someone here can teach me how to fish?" he asked, turning to Abrax.

"Well, I think you won't lack in supply of those

qualified to teach you," Abrax answered trying not to be amused by this boy. "I need to be getting back to my own home now. I'll be back to check up on you and make sure you're staying in line."

"Thanks again for helping me. I promise I'll be a good neighbor and I'll do good here," Bolek said determinedly as he felt his gratitude fill him again.

"That would be wise. This is a sacred place to me, and I have no idea why I'm allowing you to be here. But should you cause problems, I would suggest returning to the Volos because there is nowhere else you will be safe," Abrax warned, his eyes aflame.

Bolek nodded, realizing this was his chance to prove what he had been trying to prove to himself for so long—the Volos were not bad, their choices are.

"You know I don't believe what you said," Bolek said before Abrax departed.

"About what?" Abrax asked tightly.

"You are a good Solon," Bolek smiled kindly as emotion cracked his voice.

This was too much for Abrax to handle. He whispered something that Bolek was unable to hear and was gone. Bolek was glad he'd finally found out how Bright Eyes kept disappearing on him. For a while there, he thought he was quite possibly losing his mind.

Abrax appeared in his bedroom and stood

motionless, while he tried to calm his breath. He fell to his knees and sobbed as he had not sobbed in a very long time, his poor heart aching, not knowing how much more it could take.

CHAPTER NINETEEN

MORE TO LEARN

Sancia sat in a serene green sitting room waiting for her uncle and the others to come to her. She'd spent the evening quietly in her chambers. She was informed that she would meet the new guests properly that morning. Try as she may she could not remember what the other two looked like. She had been in too much of a frazzled state to notice them. The entire night, she had tossed and turned, wondering what her uncle had done. She prayed that Bolek was still alive.

The door opened and in entered first Bence, then the others, and last her uncle, to whom she paid close attention. She tried to discern any trace of what may have occurred the night before. If something drastic had happened, the remnants of it had been washed away or, more likely, buried deep.

She rose to greet the new faces. Katalin she knew and liked well. If Sancia were told to describe her in one word, it would be graceful. Her hair was golden and her eyes wise. Sancia felt she looked how a queen should look.

Ilona, on the other hand, possessed intensely sharp features with her raven hair and tan skin. She looked as though she had spent her whole life outdoors. Everything about her seemed hard until one looked into her eyes. Her sharp features were softened by her kind eyes. Sancia hoped she would get along with her.

Lastly, Sancia looked at the new man who, she had been informed, was Bence's youngest brother. He was not as tall as Bence but was built like him. His hair was dark as Bence's, but he wore no beard. His was a much more boyish face compared to Bence's.

Sancia wondered how old he was; after all he was the *youngest* brother. Her inward voice immediately warned her about her ridiculous thought, which she tended to agree with. Still, she thought he looked like someone who knew how to laugh. Not at this moment, though. He looked as though he currently might faint with her uncle at his side.

"Hi," Sancia said smiling. "I'm Sancia, welcome to Asulon."

"Thank you," Ilona responded. "I'm Ilona. You already know Katalin and the one quaking over there is Antal." Katalin tried to suppress a smirk at this description.

"I am not quaking," Antal retorted, giving Ilona look. "Hi, I'm Bence's brother," he finished, looking at Sancia. She smiled at him, and he smiled back until he remembered who stood beside him and then became very interested in his shoes.

"Sorry for bursting in like that yesterday," Sancia said. "I guess we should have given you fair warning. Now you know my form of transportation. You'll get used to it after a while, isn't that right, Bence?" she teased.

"It is not. Don't believe a word she says. You will think you are used to it and then she will prove just how wrong you were," he laughed, knowing that, although it took a great deal to startle him, she still had found a way.

"We want to thank you for your generosity in allowing us to stay here," Katalin smiled, which accentuated her regal cheek bones.

"It's our pleasure. I know Uncle Ab seems put

243

out about it, but he really likes helping people," Sancia grinned happily at him. He shook his head suppressing his own amused grin.

"Well, now that everyone has been introduced, perhaps we should get on with breakfast," Abrax suggested.

"It's ready and waiting to be served," Bence answered happily.

"We'd be lost without you, Bence," Sancia said sincerely. "Thank you for everything you do."

This took Bence by surprise. Such things were second nature to him, he did not think of them as a service deserving of gratitude.

"It's my pleasure," he answered kindly.

Abrax stood pondering over the thanks Sancia had just expressed. For so long, he had thought of both Bence's and Gergo's service to him as repaying him for the great service he had long ago rendered. How foolish to keep tabs on service from one to another.

He realized this lack of gratitude for Bence had rendered him blind to all the man did for him. True, Abrax did much for Bence as well, but Bence *always* expressed his gratitude by both word and deed. Perhaps it was time for Abrax to do the same.

"Yes, thank you, Bence," he added gruffly.

"Thank you, Abrax," Bence said. It was the first time in a very long time Bence had not called him Master.

Abrax nodded, realizing how much better he liked having his friend treat him as a friend, rather than a superior. He also discovered how much he himself was changed. He'd worked so hard to obtain the title and reputation of Master Abrax. It had been so important for so long. Ever so slowly, he was realizing perhaps being Master was not as important as being Abrax.

They breakfasted under a large white canopy that had been set up earlier alongside a lovely little pond covered with white lilies. Elek joined them and stayed at Sancia's side the whole time. Ilona was enamored of him and his magnificence. He ignored this attention, feeling she should be showing her attentions to her King.

After breakfast was over, Sancia and Elek went for a ride. Both liked running almost as much as flying but agreed flying would simply be showing off. The others watched the two in their merriment. Katalin left the others to explore the grounds. Abrax followed her and soon was at her side.

"Why do you keep these grounds so silent?" Katalin asked. "What harm is there in the song of a bird or the prance of a doe?"

"It's not the noise but the animals themselves I lock out."

"Why?" Katalin asked sadly, thinking of the effort put forth into the creation of these.

"The Volos," Abrax answered simply.

"Aw," Katalin nodded as she gained understanding. "Because there is no way to tell the difference between a true animal and a Volos replicating one."

"None that I have discovered for my eyes," Abrax answered. "Until then, the only thing in these woods will be my dogs."

"Couldn't a Volos replicate one of them?"

"They could but I would know they were not one of *my* dogs," he smiled.

She looked down at him, realizing there was something more to his statement. She readily embraced she would remain ignorant to this something more, and let it pass. It both surprised and honored her he'd come to walk with her.

"Tell me, how close were Andor and Antal before you were imprisoned?" Abrax asked, changing the subject.

"They fell out long before that time," Katalin answered remembering back. "Andor's counsel to Bence never sat right with Antal. Not because he didn't agree with it —because at the time he did; rather, because he knew Andor's counsel was not his own but someone else's. Andor isn't particularly good at originality," she smiled, thinking of her former admirer.

"Whose counsel did Antal think it was?" Abrax asked intrigued.

"He wasn't sure. He went on every one of Andor's escapades to find the answer. It didn't take long for him to find that at night Andor would wander off from the camp alone. Antal discovered him talking to a large bat and the bat would talk back."

"The Volos," Abrax stated, somewhat amused at receiving confirmation to one of his presumptions.

"Yes. Apparently, with some digging on Antal's part, he discovered Andor had fallen in with none other than the Volos King's only son. This new friendship caused no real harm until Andor was taken to King Kir himself. This was when he was given the idea of the Artur being capable of *so much more*," she scoffed disgusted. "Of course, he kept all this quiet, as the Artur were still siding with the Solon. All he had to do was wait for the seed to take root and the rest is history," she finished sadly.

"Did Andor know Antal discovered his secret?"

"Yes. Antal confronted him about it; but, by that time, my people were so calloused, the revelation was only a small irritation. They had been inwardly sided with the Volos for so long, it was only a matter of time until they outwardly were so," she answered bitterly. "Andor tried to undermine Antal so he could get rid of him. Fortunately, he only proved Antal to be the cleverer of the two."

An amused look spread through her face, but she said no more.

This information soothed Abrax's mind, knowing Antal would likely not have known of Andor's obsession with Sancia.

"How long were you imprisoned?" Abrax inquired. She gave him a sidelong glance, accompanied by an entertained smile.

"My, you are inquisitive, aren't you? I suppose I should expect no less from a Solon."

"I suppose it comes with the territory," he smiled good naturedly.

"I was put in the cellar twelve years ago," she answered.

"It took twelve years for you to get through to Ilona?" he asked sympathetically.

"Yes. I have to admit it seemed a pretty hopeless existence, spending my days talking to rocks. It was worth every bleak moment, though. Ilona was the most recent to be turned to stone. I suppose you could say she was the most connected to her true self," she said, thinking of the moment Ilona had burst from her stone state. "I think it would take a much longer time for the others to come back, if it's even possible for them to come back."

"It is always possible for them to come back," he answered softly. She looked at this man she had feared for such a long time. It was true; there were parts of him to fear, but there were also parts of him to revere.

"Thank you for trying to help my people and for helping my King," she spoke humbly.

"Bence has helped me in as many ways as I have helped him," he answered, shrugging off her thanks.

"A true friendship," she smiled.

"You are a remarkable woman, Katalin," Abrax stopped, staring up at her with what seemed to her his all-seeing eyes. "Bence is a blessed man to have such a woman's heart, even if he is unaware of the fact," she blushed as she turned away from him. "You both deserve to be happy, and I think you will be one day," he remarked turning to go, but hesitated. "That day is perhaps farther than nearer."

"I know how to wait," she whispered softly with her eyes downcast.

He left her, his respect for her growing even more. He saw Bence looking towards him but not at him. His gaze was upon a much lovelier frame than Ab's. Ab smiled as he saw the hope and the start of something greater in his friend's eyes. He saw Ilona had taken up in a race with Sancia and Elek. Antal stood at the finish line with his hands in the air to signal the takeoff.

Ab watched as Bence left the canopy and started walking in the direction of Katalin, whose course was leading her away from the others. He stood, taking in this scene before him. His eyes fell on Sancia, whose thick mahogany hair whipped in the wind. He chuckled at her laughter as she shouted excitedly for Elek to go faster.

For Ab this was enough. He thought back to the look in Bence's eyes as he gazed at Katalin and wondered if such a look would be possible in his own eyes. He shook this off. What a foolish notion. He had more important things to occupy his mind than such unrealistic qualms. He knew the foreboding future ahead of them and yet, Katalin's words still echoed in his mind . . . *I know how to wait.* Perhaps there were still one or two more things for him to learn.

CHAPTER TWENTY

IMPACT LIVES ON

Bolek, ready to explore this new place, carefully closed the door to his new home behind him. He walked with a broad grin on his face as he waved to those he passed. He looked down to the Sea and saw men preparing their ships to go out to Sea.

This is the place for me, Bolek smiled inwardly, seeing these people were *his* kind of people. He liked Redivivus, but it was a little too large for his taste. People were in such a frenzy all the time. These people here had work to do but seemed to enjoy it much more.

Bolek walked down to a few men repairing nets

who looked as burly as he did.

"Morning," he called enthusiastically.

"Mornin'," they answered back.

"Would you look at this boy?" one of them said to the other. "Brawny as a bear."

Bolek grinned good-naturedly as he set himself beside the man speaking and said, "I'm new around here and I was wondering if you knew of anyone who could teach me how to fish?"

All the men turned to the lad and laughed heartily at his question.

"Well, you've come to the right place to learn," the same man spoke.

"What's your name, son?"

"Bo. . ." Bolek answered, remembering the advice he had been given not to share his name.

"Good to meet you, Bo. I'm Bramley; this here's my brother Bristol," Bramley pointed to the man next to him; "and that one's Delton."

Both men nodded as they were introduced. Each man's face was weathered from a constant life under the sun and upon the Sea.

"Where'd you come from?" Bramley asked.

"Redivivus," Bo answered immediately.

"That's a mighty long journey," Delton remarked.

"It didn't seem very long," Bo answered smiling.

252

"Nothing seems very long when you're your age," Bristol chuckled kindly.

"So you came her to learn how to fish, did you?" Bramley smirked. He was the oldest man of the bunch, in his mid-fifties.

"Yeah. I think it looks like a fine way to make a living."

"You never said a truer word, boy," Bristol said proudly. "We're not takin'out to Sea today because we've some nets to mend. If you'd like, we could teach you?"

"I'd like that very much!" he answered happily and then asked, "Do fishermen often mend nets?"

To which he was answered with a great roar of laughter from the men, who all nodded that yes, fishermen often mended nets.

Bo watched the men closely as they showed him the proper technique to mend a net. He noticed each man added his own flare to the basic technique. He realized it was more than just a skill to them—it was an art.

They tossed him a small net to meddle with. He went much slower than the others and had to untie many knots and redo them. The men talked with him good-naturedly and encouraged him, although he made mistakes, which he appreciated.

Once he began to get the hang of it, he tried

adding his own flare to his still premature technique. Bramley eyed him humorously as he saw the boy trying hard to make his knots different than Bramley's and the others.

"You've got the right idea, but you're goin' about it the wrong way," he smiled, seeing the boy's frustrations mounting.

"What do you mean?" Bo asked looking up for guidance.

"You have to learn to do somethin' well before you can change it," he taught kindly, knowing well of what he spoke.

Bo sat, contemplating the man's words as he returned once again to the simple technique.

"Don't worry. It comes with time," Bramley encouraged. "You should've seen the first net Bristol did."

"Easy there, let's not start pointin' fingers. You've practically a collection of your own mishaps," Bristol answered.

"Don't you two start at it already—you'll scare the poor boy off before he's finished my net," Delton quipped, having grown up next door to the brothers and long ago been adopted in.

"This takes a lot of patience, doesn't it? Bo asked with his brow knit in concentration.

"Yes. Bein' around these two takes all the patience in the world,"Delton smirked.

"Oh, look who's become the innocent one?" Bristol jibbed.

"Perhaps we should move over so there's enough room for his mounds of patience," Bramley joined.

"You see what I've to put up with, Bo?" Delton looked to Bo for sympathy.

"I believe Bo was referrin' to patience in weaving and mendin', and to answer your question, yes, it does take a great deal of patience." Bramley said to Bo, "You'll learn soon enough bein' a fisherman is bein' a patient man."

"Why, that was practically poetic," Bristol joked.

"Well, consider the source," Bramley smirked.

Delton and Bristol rolled their eyes and shook their heads in unison. Bolek laughed heartily, liking these men more and more.

"You whooo!" a lady called out from behind them to which all turned and found a happy-looking woman coming towards them.

"You whooo!" the men all shouted back, trying to match her high voice.

"That's my wife, Emylynn," Bristol informed Bo cheerfully.

"I see you've captured more than fish today," she

smiled, looking down at Bolek.

"He's better than fish. He doesn't break nets, he mends 'em," Bristol answered.

"Hi, I'm Bo," Bo said up to the kindly face, which was plump and witty.

"Well, you're a sight for sore eyes, Bo. You stick out like a beacon among these wrinkles."

"He's too young for you, Emy," Bramley teased back.

"Let's not be forgettin' your current husband neither," Bristol added.

"Did you come over here just to get a closer look?" Delton charged.

"Well, I won't say it didn't quicken my step," she beamed. "But my true reason for interruptin' your work was to tell you we've changed to havin' noonmeal at our place instead of yours, Bramley."

"I don't know if we can make the trip," Bramley pretended to be let down, even though they lived next door to one another.

"How Faye puts up with you, I'll never know," Emy shook her head, referring to Bramley's wife.

"You and I both," Bramley laughed as everyone else joined in.

"You're welcome to come to our noonmeal today if you like, Bo," Emy said tenderly to Bo.

"Thank you. I'd like that."

"You'll like it more once you've tasted Emy and Faye's cookin'," Delton said patting his protruding stomach. "But I still say my Mirabel can't be touched."

"She had rare talent to be sure," Emy smiled gently, knowing he still mourned greatly over her death, though she'd been gone ten years now.

"That she did," Delton nodded sadly.

"Well, I best be gettin' back so I can fill in Faye on our new friend," she winked to Bo and then headed off.

"Hey, what about me? Remember your husband!" Bristol shouted after her smiling. She gave him a broad grin without saying a word. "I'm startin' to feel replaced," he huffed, pretending to be downtrodden. He and Emy had been together over thirty years. They had long ago grown to a place where they trusted one another completely.

Bo sat smiling, exceedingly glad he'd been brought to this place. In his heart, he thanked once again the Solon man who had brought him here. He realized he didn't know the man's name, but he acknowledge that he had never been happier than here, sitting with these men who already treated him as they treated each other. He kept at his net while the men chatted on about the Sea and other things of which he was still ignorant but eager to learn.

257

Bo finished his net and compared it to the others' completed nets. He saw his skill had room for improvement but was pleased with his work.

"Not bad," Delton observed, examining the net. "Not bad at all. You've gotta' real talent."

"Thanks," Bo smiled pleased.

"Speakin' of bad. Did you ever come across a Master Abrax when you lived in Redivivus?" Bramley asked Bo.

"Not that I know of," Bo answered. "They say he never leaves Asulon, which I can rightly believe. You should see the size of the place. The only thing larger than it is the Mountains. Why do you ask?"

"He was a relative of a friend of mine. Achaz was his name," Bramley spoke solemnly. "Apparently, Master Abrax was his younger brother. He's passed on, you see, and his daughter Sancia was taken to this man. I often wonder what's become of the little beauty . . . You remind me of Achaz, in a way."

The other two men sat quietly, knowing the sacredness of this topic for them, but particularly for Bramley.

"How?" Bo asked curious.

"Well, he was a young man when he first came to Zacroon as well, a bit older than you, though. He came with the same goal in mind, to learn how to become a fisherman. I remember the day like it was yesterday," he smiled reminiscing. "He came strolling onto the docks just like he was born to do it. The lad practically glowed with enthusiasm. It just so happened this particular day I had not caught one blasted thing and was sour with the world. I gave him a look which would scare a Mer out of the Sea." he laughed along with the other two men at this statement, which Bo only vaguely understood.

"He didn't even flinch," Bramley went on. "He sees me there toilin' on one of my little boats and climbs in to strike up conversation. Before I can get a word out, he starts askin' me every question that could be asked about bein' a fisherman. At first, I was gruff with him, but no one could be gruff around Achaz for long. Before the day was through, the boy was my apprentice and, before the week was out, one of my dearest friends."

"What happened to him?" Bo asked quietly not knowing whether he should ask or not.

Bramley sat for a moment quietly contemplating this question and then said, "Many things happened to him. He befriended everyone who came, or fell for that matter, across his path. He fished the Seas finer than any has, or any will. He found his Jacqueline and married her and brought a child into this world with her. What happened to him, you ask? He became a man, a fisherman, and a gentle man. He lived, Bo, he *really* lived."

They all sat in silence as each contemplated the life of this man. For those who had known him, the familiar pang of loss was felt. Especially Bramley, who had held a large part in Achaz's life, heaven knows Achaz was a large part of his.

Bo sat there, wondering at the story of this man and wondering at his wonder. It was obvious the man died but the topic seemed too painful for the men to discuss. He wondered how long Achaz had been gone. From what he could tell, it seemed it had been a long while.

Bo had witnessed many deaths in his time, and he had mourned these but in a different way. He felt sorrow over them as lives lost. He had never sorrowed over the loss of a life. These men had known Achaz and loved him still, even after he was gone. This affected Bo, who had never experienced death in such a way before. It made all those deaths he witnessed that much the more tragic.

"He may be gone but his impact lives on," Bo spoke reverently.

"Well said, Bo. Well said," Bristol thanked, patting him on the back.

"Well, I'd say we can finish the rest after noonmeal," Bramley said, trying to lighten the somber mood as his mind still rested upon his departed friend. He looked at the pile of mended nets, which had outgrown the pile of damaged ones. "Why not surprise the ladies. I'm sure they are just dyin' to meet our new friend."

"That's another way Bo and Achaz are alike," Delton smiled to the brothers.

"What do you mean?" Bo asked confused.

"Achaz drove the ladies *wild*," Delton teased as he slapped his hand on Bo's back. Bo laughed along with the others and was filled with something he had never felt before. For the first time in his life, he felt like he belonged. He was no longer on the outskirts looking in; he'd been welcomed into a true home—Zacroon.

CHAPTER TWENTY-ONE

THE ALDER NAME

Ferrelous tried to help his mother clear the table, but she shooed him away, telling him his father could do it. He smiled as he watched them work alongside one another, his mother's slender frame beside his father's robust one. He had opened his presents from them earlier that morning and they had eaten breakfast together. Then sat around the table lazily, reminiscing until Alura decided the time was come for them to clean up.

It was a perfect birthday start. His mother made him a new jacket and his father had given him a gold ring with their family crest engraved in it. The symbol was a tree with a short trunk and powerful branches bursting forth from it. It had the illusion of leaves on these branches but what was most impressive about it was the intricate roots system. Ferrelous knew this to be the Alder Tree.

These roots were the glory of this tree, which could restore poor soil into rich. Ferrelous thought how similar this tree was to his father, who, over the years, had restored many a sad heart to a cheerful one.

He knew his father gave this to him as a reminder—wherever you are planted, even if it is in poor soil, you have the ability to make it rich again. He saw his mother had embroidered a version of this tree onto the breast pocket of his new coat. He was glad he had been planted into the best of soil and never desired to leave it.

"What are you thinkin' about?" Alura smiled as she handed the last wet dish to Al for drying.

"Just about what great parents I have," Ferrelous grinned back.

"Can't argue with that," Al smirked as he placed this last dish into the cupboard.

"I mean it. You have done so much and always been there for me. I've never once questioned if you loved me," Ferrelous stood, saying this to both of them. For some reason, this statement touched both of them greatly. He watched as both his parents' eyes filled with tears, which they both tried to suppress. He attributed this to him being a grown man now, no longer their little boy.

"We love you too son," Al answered roughly, grabbing him in for a bear hug. He reached out for his wife, who joined in the family hug. They all laughed happily at one another's tears, not to mention their own.

It was nearing noon, Alura realized, wishing she could stop the sun as it treaded across the sky. She wanted to shout out for it to slow down! It was going much too fast. She could almost hear the reply, *Why, I'm going on the same as I always do,* she sighed, knowing the problem was on her end, not the sun's.

"Should we take a walk or maybe go sailing?" Ferrelous asked happily.

"Let's go sailin'," Al answered, knowing they needed seclusion a walk would not give, but feeling it'd be a shame to fill their home with such sadness.

"I'll get my shawl," Alura said, rushing off to her and Al's bedroom.

Soon, they were in the midst of the Sea with a clear blue sky above them. Ferrelous lay lazily, soaking in the sun's rays, while Alura and Al watched him quietly. Neither of them wanted to break this blissful moment, which would be the last of its kind.

"Son," Al said, softly cutting into the sound of the calm breeze.

"Yeah, dad?" Ferrelous sighed without opening his eyes.

"There's somethin' your mom and I need to talk to you about."

"What's that?" he answered, raising his head slightly, eyes opened this time.

"Come sit by us," Alura said, reaching her hand out to him.

He came over confused as to why his parents were acting so somber. Neither of them was prone to serious moods. To have both of them at the same time in such a one was unheard of.

"What is it?" Ferrelous asked warily.

"Do you remember last night when we talked about my eldest brother?" Al asked.

"Yeah, sure," he answered confused.

"What do you remember?"

"You know that he was your hero and that he left on the night of his eighteenth birthday. . ." Ferrelous answered, his heart rate picking up for some reason.

"That's right, but what I didn't tell you was that my brother's name is Timeus, and he was adopted. He

265

was brought to my father and mother as a charge from a Solon man. Timeus was raised in secrecy from the world to protect both him and our world," Al explained seriously.

"What do you mean?"

"First, you must understand the Alder Tree symbol is the symbol of our family because we are the safe guarders of a Secret People. This people come from a very difficult place and an elect few are brought to us to nurture, to sink our roots in, so to speak. They are brought to us by the Solon. We raise them as our own until their eighteenth birthday. Then, the Solon come and take them back to teach them about who they truly are."

"And who are they? Truly?" Ferrelous asked, wondering who his father's brother really was.

"I don't know," Alder admitted quietly.

"You mean our family has been doing this for all these years and never discovered who they were raising?" he gawked shocked.

"It is crucial this people's existence remains secret. All I know of them is that they are here to defend this world from the immortals who fall away from the Creator. They work hand in hand with the Solon to continually save the world from these."

Ferrelous sat, in contemplation, wondering why

266

his father never discussed this with him before. He could have been preparing himself to raise one of these Secret People's for a long while now.

"Are your other brothers each raising one of these Secret People?" he asked.

"No. Only those who bare the Alder name are given such an honor," Al answered, trying to contain his emotions.

Two things entered Ferrelous's mind at this moment. First, his name was not Alder; second, his father's name was.

"Why didn't you name me Alder?" Ferrelous asked, fearful of the reply.

"Because you already had a name when you came to us," Alura answered softly, seeing that her husband couldn't answer this question.

"I'm not your son," Ferrelous whimpered, feeling his world caving in.

"You listen to me," Alura said, taking his face in her hands. "You are *our* son. We have always loved you and always will love you as such."

Ferrelous hugged her tightly to him not knowing what else to do. These were the arms he had always felt safe in, always belonged in.

"You don't know where I came from?" he asked as he pulled gently away from her.

267

"No. You were brought to us by Achaz the morning he entered Zacroon. He was the Solon whose protection you were under."

"What?" Ferrelous gasped as his mind nearly collapsed.

"Achaz was a Solon man, and he was your protector. He saved you not only because . . . well, he was Achaz, but because you were *Ferrelous.*"

"I killed him," Ferrelous groaned as his head dropped into his hands. "I killed the man whom I not only looked up to, but who was looking after *me.*"

"Many Solon have lost their lives protecting others. It is somethin' to mourn but somethin' more to revere," Al asserted as a feeling of peace came over him and reached out to the others. "They understand life is both personal and plural. They recognize why the Creator created life with each."

"If I hadn't gone out, Achaz would still be alive," Ferrelous rebuffed, trying to hold off his father's words.

"If Achaz was supposed to still be alive, he would be," Al answered. "The Solon are needed as much in the next life as in this, especially a Solon like Achaz."

"What about Sancia?" Ferrelous agonized upset.

"She was not given anythin' she couldn't handle and neither were you," Alura reassured, knowing the guilt her son carried with him.

Ferrelous sat thinking of how Sancia seemed to be content with her life, but was this because she didn't truly understand the life she had lost?

"It's time for you let go of your guilt, Ferrelous," Alura softly spoke watching him struggle. "Achaz forgave you, Jacqueline forgave you, Marceline forgave you, Sancia forgave and forgives you still. . . It's time for you to forgive yourself."

Ferrelous wept bitter tears. He had long punished himself for his crime. He felt he deserved it because of what he'd done. The realization came to him softly, almost as if someone gently placed it in his mind, that guilt is given to lead, not to haunt.

He had allowed the sacrifice of Achaz to fill his heart so fully, he had paid no attention to the result of the sacrifice. The very *reason* Achaz gave his life had escaped Ferrelous these many years. This was not honoring Achaz; this was not showing gratitude for what he had done. Achaz died so another might live. He knew what Ferrelous was capable of becoming, even though Ferrelous himself did not know.

How wrong it would be for Ferrelous to hold on to what he himself had done, instead of who he could become, who Achaz knew he held the potential to become. This was how he could show his gratitude; this was how he could honor Achaz. . . this was how he could become a man like Achaz.

"You're right, mom, as usual," he smiled as he wiped the tears away from his eyes. Alura embraced the only child she had ever known and loved.

"She's a keeper," Al smiled as he placed his arms around both his wife and son.

They sat listening to the sounds of the Sea quietly, all too exhausted to speak. This day was difficult for each in their own individual way. Yet, the only way each had been able to get through it was together.

Ferrelous did not know what his future held. He never desired anything more than what he'd already been given. He realized he had been given much and now it was time for him to give back. There was a great deal more his parents and he needed to discuss.

Many questions swirled through his mind and increased in number as the moments past, but these were secondary to what he had already obtained— The knowledge that he would always be the son of Alura and Alder, and that he would never stop trying to live up to Achaz's sacrifice. His solid foundation, which had been laid by so many, most of all his parents, had stood and would continue to do so.

"Thank you for being my parents," he whispered, holding tighter to the two people he had never dreamed he would have to let go.

"Thank you for being our son," they answered back in unison, holding onto the boy they always knew they would have to let go, but never wanted to.

CHAPTER TWENTY-TWO

LEARNING HOW TO GLEAN

Antal walked the grounds glad to have some solitude with his pulsating thoughts. He couldn't get enough of the sunlight. He lay down on the grass and felt the sun rays warm his body. A grin grew across his face, expressing just how much he had missed the sun. It made him wonder why he hadn't returned to Bence long ago. There are few things as joyful as a sunbeam.

"I like to do that too," a voice said. He looked up to see Sancia standing above him. He was so lost in the sun; he had not heard her walk up. He bounded to his feet.

"Oh, did I frighten you?" she asked.

"No, no. I just. . . wanted to stand up," he

answered nervously, keeping his eyes averted. The sunbeams hitting her hair looked dazzling.

"Oh well. . . I was just trying to find Elek when I saw you over here," she explained.

"You and Elek seem very close," he noted, relaxing some as his mind turned to the almos.

"He's like my brother. There's nothing we wouldn't do for each other. He's pretty protective of me and, well, of everyone he loves," she laughed thinking of how he treated their new guests. "He'll warm up to you all eventually."

"Does your uncle know you're out here?" Antal asked, looking around, wondering if this was some kind of test they were putting him through.

"I don't know. I haven't seen him since breakfast. He has much more to do these days than watch my every move," she answered, amused at both how her uncle was avoiding her and how nervous Antal was about her uncle. She, of course, understood the behaviors behind both men. It was amusing all the same.

"I don't think he would like us talking like this alone."

"Listen, if you're going to be staying here, we might as well be friends. I just want you to feel welcome here. You seem a little on edge . . . all the time. I guess that's why I came over. It's nice to see you unwind some."

"That's really thoughtful of you. . . it is. . . and I appreciate it. But I think it'll be best if we keep our distance from each other," he spoke slowly. He saw the hurt expression come over her face as she dropped her gaze to the ground.

"Okay. . . I'm sorry to have bothered you," she replied quietly, keeping her gaze on the ground.

Antal felt horrible and started to search for something to say. He didn't get the chance.

"Hey there!" Elek called out as he swooped in beside them.

"Hey yourself," Sancia slightly smiled as she wrapped her arms around his neck and buried her face in his mane, glad she could brush the tears forming in her eyes away unnoticed.

"What are you doing out here?" Elek asked Sancia, completely ignoring Antal.

"I was coming to find you when I saw Antal here. Let's fly," she said as she mounted him.

"Thanks for coming over to talk to me," Antal stated lamely.

She looked at him for a moment and quietly rebuked, "You shouldn't say things you don't mean."

She leaned forward in her take-off position,

signaling Elek it was time to go. He didn't hesitate as he was also ready to distance himself from this *Antal*. He speculated about her words, but didn't press for information, knowing that, right now, she desired to hear nothing but the beat of his wings.

Antal watched in wonder as they soared high above him. He jolted as he watched her leap from Elek's back, only for Elek to quickly regain his passenger. It was amazing to see the harmony of this act. It was apparent they flew together often.

Antal felt the sting of her words and the pained expression she wore when she had spoken them. He reasoned that she simply did not understand the position he was in. He would gladly be her friend if he could trust himself, it would remain just a friendship for him, or worse for her. He lay down again as he watched them do all sorts of feats.

He was wrong to speak to her in such a manner, no matter the circumstance. Perhaps that was why he felt as though he was carrying a ball of granite in his stomach. After all, it wasn't her fault he had a problem. He would apologize to her when the opportunity presented itself and extend a hand of friendship. She was right. As things were now, it would be futile to try avoiding her, even in such a massive place as Asulon. Not to mention uncomfortable.

275

"What a blubbering idiot I am," he scoffed out loud to himself.

"Well, at least you can admit it," Bence quipped smiling, walking up to his brother. "What've you done this time?"

"I told Sancia to stay away from me after she tried to offer her friendship."

"Hmmm. . ." Bence smirked, shaking his head amused. "I agree. You are a blubbering idiot."

"Thanks for that," Antal answered as he rolled his eyes, but then went on seriously. "The truth is, Bence, I'm afraid of myself. I don't know if there's anything worse than not being able to trust oneself. Do you know what it's like to look in the mirror and have all the horrific choices you've made staring back at you?"

Bence looked at his youngest brother with sadness as he watched him try and handle his pain. He could only imagine the battle constantly raging within Antal.

"I can't tell you what to do because I don't know what you're going through," Bence acknowledged as he sat beside him. "I can only say hurting Sancia isn't going to make your condition any better. I'd say it has a good chance of making it worse," he paused gathering his words and then went on. "The truth is you've learned to only look at a person's exterior and leave it there. It's an

276

easy but foolish habit to fall into. You and I both know the inner life put into any creation is its true glory."

Antal listened to these words as he thought of his own past creations, and how pointless they would be without their inner selves.

Bence went on, "Do you know why it's so hard for me to understand why Sancia's appearance affects you so? Because her greatest beauty comes from within her; honestly, it far outshines her nice hair and pretty smile. When I see her, I see Sancia, not a pretty girl whose name is Sancia. . . Maybe you should try seeing instead of just looking, brother. If you'll let yourself *see,* you will discover Sancia is far more beautiful than just a pretty girl."

The brothers sat quietly for a moment as each pondered on the words spoken. Antal always admired Bence, which had gnawed at him during his rebellion. He glanced over at the strong features that were his brother's. He saw it was the man within that made these features truly strong.

"When did you become so wise?" Antal smiled.

Bence chuckled, glad he had made his point.

"I guess that's what happens when you spend all your time around a man such as Abrax."

"No. It's more than that, Bence. You're much deeper than the influences around you. Always have been," he asserted, thinking about how, when Bence walked away, he had done so alone. Antal had not. He fled with two friends who were much better than he was.

"Give yourself a chance, Antal. We've all made mistakes, and we all regret them. The point is to learn from them. That's the only way we ever rise above them," Bence said as he stood to leave. "I think you are wise to be cautious around Sancia, but you could learn a great deal from her and she from you."

Antal watched as his brother walked away, wondering what Bence meant. What could he learn from a fourteen-year-old girl? Age gleans wisdom. Doesn't it? Yet, he had noticed over his lifetime that there are those born excellent gleaners while others must learn how to glean.

He thought over this concept as he began to walk back to the house. It would be dinner soon. He could only imagine how it would go now he'd successfully slapped Sancia's kindness away. He saw her and Elek land a ways in front of him.

"Better now than never," he muttered, knowing well the path of procrastination.

"Sancia, may I have a word?" he shouted. She stared at him and Elek said something to her, which made her smile, but she shook her head to indicate a negative. Antal waited to see what she would do. He wouldn't blame her if she told him he could take his word and shove it back down his throat.

She didn't, however. She simply walked, somewhat stoically, toward him.

"Yes?" she asked politely.

"I just wanted to say I'm sorry about what I said earlier. I don't want to make excuses for myself. I just want you to know that I'm in the process of changing the person I was and am. I was afraid you'd be an obstacle to that change, but Bence helped me see that you're probably a person who could help guide me through it. That is, if you'll accept my apology and my friendship?" he asked, looking humbled and sincere as he waited for her to respond.

She waited for a moment but then let out a sigh and smiled looking at him, "We really need to work on your people skills."

"Add it to the list," he grinned as the granite ball eased itself out of his gut.

"Are you coming?" Elek shouted impatiently, observing these goings-on from his distant post.

"Yeah, *we're* coming," Sancia shouted back, giving Antal an amused look at Elek consistently ignoring his presence.

"Doesn't like me much, does he?" Antal smiled.

"Give it time. Elek and my uncle are similar in that way."

"You mean how they both don't like me?" he joked.

"Well, that," she smirked. "And they don't give their trust. It has to be earned."

"And what about you? What is your trust status?" he asked lightly.

"I trust the good in a person more than the bad, unless I discover the latter is stronger."

Antal hadn't expected this response. It rendered him silent for a moment as he considered her words.

"Elek is fortunate to have you as a sister," he said, thinking on how he'd lacked in his duties to his eldest brother. He had spent a much longer lifetime with Bence than Sancia had spent with Elek. Yet, it seemed she held a much better understanding of her brother. "You know what I think?" he asked.

"That Elek is fortunate to have me?"

"Well, that, and that you are a born gleaner," he informed her, looking down at her knowingly, "while I'm still learning how to glean."

"What are you talking about?" she laughed, knowing he knew she was ignorant of what he was talking about.

"I'll tell you later," he mumbled as they neared

Elek.

"Would you hurry it up? It's almost dinner time and you know how Master Abrax is about his mealtimes."

"Oh Elek, you're such a quirk," Sancia laughed as she kissed his soft nose.

The three walked together as Sancia spoke with both Elek and Antal. Antal attempted conversation with Elek, which was denied. Elek left them when they entered the house with Katalin. He could tolerate her and even extended a greeting.

They entered Abrax's favorite Dining Hall and saw he'd already begun his meal along with Ilona who was enthralled by her food. Sancia was reminded of her uncle's avoidance of her. She knew he didn't want to discuss what happened with Bolek. Hide as he may, he would have to tell her sometime; she hoped it would happen after dinner.

"Good. You're all here," Abrax said as Bence also entered, "I have an announcement to make which will affect all of you."

"What is it?" Sancia asked intrigued.

"Later this evening, we will be joined by another guest. I must stress his presence being kept an absolute secret. I hope you *all* realize I am showing the level of trust I have in each of you. I advise for each involved, it not be broken," he stated calmly.

"Who are you bringing here?" Sancia inquired shocked. *Could it be Bolek?*

He gazed at her inquisitive face amused, seeing traces of Achaz. He knew full well she wouldn't rest until she knew. He didn't see the harm in it as she and Bence were the only ones aware of whom Ferrelous was, without knowing *who* Ferrelous was.

"Ferrelous," he answered, as a smile crept to the corners of his mouth awaiting her response.

"*Ferrelous?*" she gasped, almost falling off her chair. She would have expected Bibi before she would have expected Ferrelous to enter this house. "As in, of Zacroon?"

"Correct," Abrax answered, as a broad smile appeared while watching her mind whizzing.

"Ferrelous?" she repeated as though she hadn't heard him correctly.

"Yes, my dear. Ferrelous, friend of Audric, former beau of Bibi, and son of Alder and Alura of Zacroon."

"Why in the name of common sense would you bring him here?" she asked baffled.

"I'm going to teach him, and we'll end it right there for now," he established, giving her the look he gave her when he meant what he said.

"Yeah, okay. But Bibi's never going to speak to

me again," Sancia muttered falling to the back of her chair.

Abrax burst out in a bellow of laughter. It never ceased to amaze him the things that came out of Sancia's mind and mouth. The newcomers to the table sat in awe as they witnessed this miracle of mirth before them. Sancia and Bence joined in the laughter while the others sat in shock.

Antal gazed upon his newfound friend and realized this was no regular fourteen-year-old girl. He now better understood Bence's former wise words to him. Anyone with the ability to cause a fit of laughter in Master Abrax had a great deal of knowledge he had yet to acquire. He was most ready to glean from this born gleaner.

CHAPTER TWENTY-THREE

FERRELOUS'S FAREWELL

Ferrelous sat by the fireplace with his parents on each side of him. Al was in the middle of telling one of his favorite memories of Ferrelous as a boy. Alura and Ferrelous grinned, recalling the outlandish moment. They had finished dinner and Alura decided they could clean up later. An all-time first in their household. They heard a knock at the door, which wiped the joviality from their faces.

Come in," Al called without removing himself from the side of his son.

The door opened and in entered Master Abrax silently. He stared at the little family, who gazed back at him. His eyes fell on Ferrelous, who looked at him with so many emotions, he could not decipher how the boy had taken the news.

"We didn't realize the time," Alura explained, trying to suppress her sadness.

"I'll go get my things," Ferrelous said, without waiting for Abrax's reply, as he went to his room for the last time. He put on his new jacket; he was already wearing his ring. He grabbed a bundle containing all he would be taking with him, the few reminders he would have left of home. He stood for a moment, looking around his room, then let out a long breath as he gently closed the door behind him.

When he re-entered the main room, his parents were standing with their arms around each other for support. He swallowed hard, knowing how difficult this must be for them. He set his bundle down and walked over to embrace them tightly.

"I love you. I *will* come home someday," he promised determinedly.

"We'll always be here for you," Alura answered softly.

"*Always*," Al nodded as his tears fell freely, knowing there was a great chance his son would never come home again.

"It's time to go, Ferrelous," Abrax interjected.

Ferrelous pulled back from his parents to get

one last look. How many times had he taken the chance to look at them for granted? His mother's sweet face alongside his father's jovial one. They smiled at him proud of the man he had become.

"You'll never know how much you both mean to me. You're the greatest parents anyone could ask for," Ferrelous sobbed, as his emotions got the best of him. "Thank you for puttin' up with me and lovin' me," he finished, purposefully sliding back into his fisherman twang.

"We love you, son," Al answered as he pulled Ferrelous in for one last embrace.

Abrax stood, quietly observing the moving scene before him. Ferrelous quickly kissed his mother's forehead, then clapped his arms around his father's neck. He walked over to Abrax, trying to brace his wretched state.

"I'm ready," he said still gazing at his parents, who were attempting to smile bravely at him.

Abrax nodded and picked up the bundle Ferrelous had forgotten. Alura and Al chuckled, causing Ferrelous to grin his familiar boyish grin. Abrax handed part of the cloak to Ferrelous. Ferrelous took it questioningly. He locked his eyes on his parents, feeling the farewell at hand. They smiled through their flowing tears.

"Asulon, library," Abrax uttered softly as he watched Ferrelous's eyes clinging to his parents. Alura and Al clung to each other as their son disappeared before their eyes. They knelt to the ground, unable to bear the weight of this loss. They sat, clutching one another as their tears joined in one sorrow. Marriage had unified their two hearts in their bliss, their sorrow, and everything in-between.

Ferrelous and Ab appeared in the library. Ferrelous gasped, looking around at this new place flashing before his eyes. His parents were nowhere to be seen. His head dropped as tears speckled the unfamiliar floor beneath him.

"Will I ever see them again?" he asked softly.

"That depends on you," Abrax answered.

"What do you mean?" he asked.

"It means anything is possible to the person who never stops trying," Ab answered as he removed the cloak and set it on his favorite chair.

Ferrelous sat taking in this statement as his thoughts returned to his parents. They would never stop trying for him. He was their son and would never stop trying for them. He hoped they were alright and wondered how his abrupt departure had impacted them. He couldn't imagine and, what's more, he didn't want to.

"So, what now?" Ferrelous asked, wiping the tears away he couldn't stop producing.

"Now I will take you to your room. I think you've taken in quite enough for one day," he answered bidding Ferrelous to follow him. They walked through the halls of the mansion in silence as Ferrelous gaped at the grandeur. It rivaled the Mer city.

Sancia came out of a room as they were walking towards it.

"What are you doing?" Abrax sighed exasperatedly, realizing he should have reiterated that she not welcome Ferrelous earlier this morning. He had explained that Ferreluos would be in a state of severe mourning and distress upon his arrival. He thought this would be enough for her. Now he realized it only stressed upon her the need of being here to comfort and help her friend.

"I was double-checking his room to make sure everything was suitable," came her ready reply.

Ferrelous had forgotten this was Sancia's home. It was startling for him to see her, not to mention embarrassing. He quickly brushed his tears away and tried to avoid eye contact.

"Hi Ferrelous," she whispered kindly, walking up to him and giving him a hug. "I'm so sorry about all

288

this."

He hugged her back; now glad she had come. She was the only familiar thing to him in this place.

"Thanks Sancia," he whispered back.

She pulled away as her own eyes filled with emotion, seeing the intense pain of her friend and feeling some of it herself.

"Your room is right here and,well, I had Bence make a few changes so it would be a little more . . . like you," she smiled as she took his hand leading the way.

This information was news to Abrax who wondered what the deuce she had done to his . . . *their* house. They entered the room, which now was filled with the distinct aroma of the Sea. The room looked like a large cottage bedroom. The headboard, which was before a large intricate gold one, had been replaced with a glazed wood one with a ship carved into it. Abrax chuckled quietly, shaking his head at his niece's blasted consideration.

"Well done," Ab muttered, giving her one of his amused looks, to which she smiled cheekily.

"This is wonderful," Ferrelous was in awe, feeling that he would sleep much better here than any other room in this massive place. "Thank you."

"You're welcome," Sancia smiled in her triumph. "If you need anything else, let me know," she quickly hugged him once more, "I'll see you at breakfast."

She walked to her uncle who stood a few feet away.

He whispered seriously, "Bibi's going to be furious."

"If you don't tell, I won't," she giggled as she gave him a peck on the cheek good night. He smiled as he kissed her forehead, and she left the room.

"Can I ask you something?" Ferrelous questioned.

"I don't see why not," Abrax answered, becoming more serious.

"Why did you take over for Achaz? I mean after what I did?" he asked.

"You were important to him. He's the only Solon I know of who has resided in the same town as the person they were in charge of," Abrax answered, considering this fact for the thousandth time. "It's interesting you should phrase it as what you did. You were not old enough to be held accountable, and yet, you held yourself accountable. I have held a respect for you for a very long time, Ferrelous," Abrax clarified, observing the young man's miserable countenance. "You have become a man, which is what Achaz desired and why he willingly gave his life. Achaz's death is not in vain because you are living up to the responsibility it has placed on you."

"I still have a long way to go," Ferrelous answered firmly.

"We all do," Abrax replied to this young man, who had grown from a distance before his eyes. He looked forward to getting to know him better.

Achaz had seen a great deal in this boy, even from his infancy. Ferrelous was born destined for greatness. Achaz's death helped the seed of this to flourish within the child. It had been a sacrifice Achaz was willing to make and Abrax was learning to appreciate, hard as that may be.

"Good night Ferrelous."

"Good night. . ." Ferrelous faltered, realizing he wasn't sure what to call this man.

"Abrax. . . just Abrax," he put forth, answering his dilemma.

"Good night, Abrax," Ferrelous tried to smile as he watched Abrax leave his room. He gazed around his new residence and wondered what his room looked like before. He could tell by Abrax's reaction it was now very different from what it had formerly been before Sancia took over.

He remembered his mother's words about how thoughtful Sancia was, how mature. He was more thankful for her friendship today than he'd ever been. She had been so kind to him in a situation that could have been very awkward for them both.

He heard a light tap on his door and walked over to open it. There was Sancia again. He smiled down at her upturned smiling face.

"Hi, I was just thinking about how sad your parents must be about all this. That got me thinking about my own parents and how having paintings of them has helped me so much. So, I was wondering if it would be alright with you if I painted a portrait of you for them?" she rattled this off very quickly as she wasn't sure if she was overstepping her bounds. "I like to paint, like my mother did, and I'm getting better at it."

Ferrelous stood gazing at her, then stepped forward and hugged her tightly.

"Thank you, Sancia. You have no idea what that would mean to me and to them."

"Oh, it's not a big deal. I just thought it might help," she answered happily. "I'd like to have you sit for it, though. I want it to be as lifelike as possible. I don't know how good it will be, but I'd like at least to give it a try."

"I'm sure it will be amazing. I saw the portrait of

you and your uncle in the library with your signature on it," he answered.

"Oh well, I guess I'll let you go to sleep now. I just couldn't wait until morning," she admitted embarrassed.

"I'm glad you didn't. Good night," he replied graciously. He watched her walk down the hall and quickly wave as she turned the corner. He stood there after she had gone, feeling again how glad he was that she was here. He thought of Timeus and how he had been so harsh towards him for leaving his family.

His feelings were greatly changed towards this man. He wondered where he was now. He wondered what had kept him away from returning to the family he'd loved and who loved him. He thought of his father having to go through this goodbye twice.

He walked out onto the veranda which adjoined his new room. He stared out across the yard and saw a large animal walking across it in the moonlight. He'd never seen such a creature before. Part lion, part bird, part horse. He was sure this must be Elek, whom he had heard so much about. He'd been sworn to secrecy by Bibi, who was the informant about Sancia's adopted brother. He had to admit he hadn't believed her fully at the time. He wondered how Bibi would react when she found out about his new residency. The thought made him shudder slightly.

Elek looked up at him and nodded a salutation. Ferrelous waved back, wondering what other spectaculars this place held. He returned indoors and sat down upon his bed. Exhaustion weighed upon him from the strain of the day, but he found himself unable to relax enough for sleep.

He finally lay down under the covers as his mind continued to flurry around in commotion. In the darkness, his thoughts became more clear and vibrant. He found that, amongst all the chaos, his mind always came back to the same three questions.

Who am I? Where did I come from? What am I supposed to do now? Today brought these questions and tomorrow would answer them. He wasn't sure which was more frightening —the questions or the answers. He felt a deep loneliness come over him as he lay in this unfamiliar place. He thought of his parents and the life he would never have with them.

A new wave of tears escaped, wetting his pillow as this loneliness crushed him further and deeper. He tossed and turned until, for some unknown reason, his thoughts rested on Achaz.

He felt a peace wash over him as if Achaz was in the room, telling him everything would be alright. He hadn't stopped protecting Ferrelous. He was not alone. Marceline's words floated through him after all these years — *I only thought I was alone. Think of it, I had that whole family right there by me all this time and I felt alone because I couldn't see them. It's the same with our loved ones who die. We can't see them, but they are always there, right by us.*

"Thank you," Ferrelous whispered into the darkness as gratitude filled him, making him feel light. He could almost feel a smile in response as he drifted off into a peaceful slumber, now ready for what the future would bring.

Sancia, on the other hand, still couldn't sleep. No one had seen her work except her family here in Asulon. Of course, *they'd* told her it was good. She was pleased to hear Ferrelous also thought so. Still, he could have just tried to be nice out of consideration for her offer.

She realized her uncle hadn't returned her cloak to her. He must have forgotten with all the drama of the evening. She quietly left her room, making her way down to the library where she was certain it would be. The house was silent as everyone was now sleeping, or so she supposed.

As she neared the library door, she heard voices coming from within. The first she didn't recognize, but the second she did.

"You're sure you won't change your mind?" a rich

female voice asked.

"Entirely," Abrax replied.

"It is very unorthodox. No human has been instructed anywhere but in Solon City," the female voice stressed, faintly worried, "and Timeus is *anxious* to meet him."

"You and I both know I'm rather well known for my unorthodox manner," Abrax quipped. "You also know my stance on *Timeus*. The man responsible for my father's death should remain in Solon City, where he and I won't have a chance of meeting *again.*"

Sancia heard the dangerous tone her uncle's voice had taken on. She hoped the lady wouldn't push the subject any further.

"This is your final word?" the woman asked.

"Indeed," Abrax responded decisively. "Should Timeus come here. . ." he began.

"He won't," she cut in.

He waited patiently for her explanation, knowing it must be an excellent one for her to be so definite on the matter.

"Not only because of your being here, but we have recently discovered that his son is living in Redivivus," she whispered this last piece, making Sancia strain to hear.

"Kaius is in Redivivus?" he asked, taken aback.

"Yes," she answered fervently.

"Remarkable," Abrax said digesting this news.

"You're sure you won't reconsider your stance on Ferrelous?" she asked gently.

"Absolutely not," he affirmed, more determined than ever.

"Very well then. I will return to report, but I must stress once again, Abrax, Ferrelous is no ordinary human."

Sancia, as silently as she could, slipped away before the conversation came to a close and she was caught by one or the other. Obviously, this had been meant to be a secret meeting, which she should not have overheard. She was impressed with the idea that Uncle Ab was losing in his resolution to shut the world out and be tucked away. This thought opened the door to others.

She pondered who the woman was and what she looked like. She marveled at this Timeus, the reason for her grandfather's death, and also his neighboring son Kauis; but above all, she wondered what a *human* was. . .?

Printed in Great Britain
by Amazon

42711954R00165